Doughnut Books
Portland, Oregon
doughnut-books.com

ISBN (paperback) 979-8-9888154-9-5

Cover design and interior formatting by FZ Boda

Heroin Anonymous World Service Conference-Approved literature. All stories contributed by members of the fellowship of Heroin Anonymous.

Heroin Anonymous

NO MORE SUFFERING

First Edition

TABLE OF CONTENTS

Introduction

This section describes where H.A. comes from, who
we aim to help, and the purpose of this book.

PREFACE

The purpose of the book *Heroin Anonymous* is to describe our fellowship and to share the experience of people whose lives were saved from the grips of heroin and opioid addiction by Heroin Anonymous (H.A.). Our membership and the groups they comprise come from many walks of life. Yet, our similarities, rather than our differences, bind us together into a powerful force for change. This book honors our diversity while also identifying our common qualities.

Many of us have found that this sense of mutual identification is invaluable when we share our success with others as an example of what is possible for the suffering addict. In the same sentiment, we have found it necessary to compile this book.

The biggest challenge in writing a book like *Heroin Anonymous* was the attempt to capture our core identity as it exists *today*. Despite our limitations, a valuable aspect of our character lies in our readiness to embrace innovation. We hope that individuals who find their own success from H.A. build upon what we have offered here. When we share freely what we've been given, we can not only help those who are as desperate for relief as we once were, but we can also ensure our own sobriety in the process.

In 2022, the Heroin Anonymous World Service Conference requested that a task force be formed to explore whether the fellowship would benefit from a book – and if so, what kind of text would best serve its members. The committee conducted a survey of the H.A. fellowship, and the result was clear: a resounding "yes." The fellowship expressed a strong desire for a book that reflected their experiences, history, and traditions. It was also vital to have a book that would serve both those already within the fellowship and those still suffering who had yet to find us.

The task force, composed of passionate members from different regions and one non-heroin addict advisor, took on the responsibility of shaping a vision for this book using the responses received from the survey. Importantly, the book needed to represent the lived experiences of H.A. members. The fellowship also conveyed that it had no desire to develop a replacement for the book *Alcoholics Anonymous*, which is widely used by members and was approved at the 2018 World Service Conference as an official resource for the fellowship.

Following the 2023 Heroin Anonymous World Service Conference, the fellowship formally requested the development of a book, charging the Heroin Anonymous World Services Inc. Board of Directors with assembling a dedicated committee to produce a rough draft to present at the 2025 World Service Conference. The group responsible for this work came together with a shared purpose: to create a text that embodies the spirit of H.A. while remaining true to its principles. This book was built on the collective voices of our membership – people from different backgrounds, locations, and experiences – all united by the common goal of staying sober and helping others to sobriety.

The content of this book reflects the input of the fellowship itself; based on the survey approved at the 2022 World Service Conference, the most requested elements were personal stories, insights into our history, our 12 Traditions, and experiences with the 12 Steps. By honoring these requests, we have sought to capture deeply personal experiences that are relatable to those who have directly or indirectly experienced the illness of heroin or opioid addiction. This book is meant to serve the suffering addict, and to inform members of the public and professional community who wish to better understand our purpose.

If you are struggling with heroin or opioid addiction, you are not alone. There is a solution; there is a way out.

FOREWORD

An introduction to our fellowship, its history, and its pioneering members.

The history of Heroin Anonymous is, of course, tightly bound to heroin use. In the late 2000s, changing drug laws and limits on prescription opioids in the United States corresponded with an increase in heroin use. Although the use of heroin has fluctuated over time, it has never disappeared, and opioids remain prevalent today in different forms.

Considering that many individuals were in their late teens and early twenties during the popularization of heroin in the late 2000s, it is unsurprising that H.A.'s membership was primarily people in their mid-to-late twenties for the first decade of the society's existence. Over time, this generalization has applied less to our fellowship, which is now more diverse in age, race, gender, and many other dimensions. While our fellowship still contains a considerable number of young people, it also contains a substantial fraction of older individuals, many of whom have long-term sobriety and experience. This book is for all of them, and all of us – just as the fellowship and the 12 Steps are for anyone who wants them.

Heroin Anonymous was born from a deep respect for the principles of Alcoholics Anonymous. Some of our early members got sober in A.A. and were familiar not only with the A.A. steps, but also their traditions, concepts, and overall service structure. As heroin addicts, our pioneering members recognized that their recovery was limited within A.A.'s Singleness of Purpose. In a broad view, Singleness of Purpose is the idea that a 12-Step fellowship should keep its focus on a particular substance, behavior, or problem. This meant that heroin addicts attending A.A. sometimes had trouble relating to the message shared in meetings or were even asked to leave. They also felt that how they carried the message was incomplete and sometimes even dishonest, due to their avoidance of sharing specifically about heroin. After all, "the feeling of having shared in a common peril is one element in the powerful cement which binds us," as stated in the book *Alcoholics Anonymous.* A need was indicated. The conditions for H.A.'s birth were created.

On July 26, 2004, Paul F., a sober heroin addict in A.A., received a phone call from another heroin addict. Paul was asked, "How come there is no Heroin Anonymous?" At that moment, Paul decided to start H.A. so heroin addicts could be with others who truly understood the experience of heroin addiction. Fliers were distributed to heroin addicts in other 12-Step fellowships, and they found several people who were also enthusiastic about having their own program. On July 28, 2004, Paul and six others held the first meeting of Heroin Anonymous at a halfway house in Phoenix, Arizona. At that first meeting, Paul was elected as the literature chairperson and soon began writing pamphlets and meeting formats for the budding fellowship. Though members of H.A. recall other early meetings taking place in Arizona, Texas, and Colorado, it was this group in Phoenix where H.A. really caught fire, making it the birthplace of Heroin Anonymous. Not long after that first meeting in July, other meetings started to form, and Phoenix's H.A. Intergroup was established on November 11, 2004.

Paul F. was initially the driving force behind

the fellowship's formation; today, he is considered the founder of H.A. Paul was a passionate and motivated individual. He was known for being a fierce advocate and was dedicated to helping the fellowship expand while still adhering to our Traditions.

Paul's vision for a sustainable fellowship is one of the reasons that H.A. has survived and has continued to flourish for more than two decades. Paul and the other founders had the foresight to quickly form a service structure for H.A. as a skeleton for future growth. This included meetings, the Phoenix Area Intergroup, and World Services. At first, this seemed like overkill, since the membership was small, and the people involved in service were Phoenix locals. Paul and others contributed their time and energy, but it was clear that something more than individual determination was needed. While Paul's contribution was substantial, it took many people to help start our society – and grow it.

Without these founding members' involvement, how could H.A. function? Most of these members only had a few years sober, and many had even less than a year. At that time, our fellowship had been operating as a typical organization: the World Services Board was at the top, telling the groups below it how to function. Notably, this was the opposite of how A.A. and other fellowships organized themselves, where groups are at the top of the service structure and pass recommendations to lower service levels. The purpose of each lower service level is simply to serve the one above it. This tried-and-true structure, known as the "inverted triangle," is a treasured part of A.A.'s operation, and in many ways is thought to have allowed for A.A.'s longevity.

Despite H.A.'s challenges early on, and even fear at times, our organization was able to adapt to its own changing needs as our membership rapidly increased. Instead of treading water, afraid of the great depth below, the fellowship's changes forced us to swim with the current. In other words, conceptually, the triangle service structure of H.A. had begun to invert, and rightly so.

Over time, we have expanded and organized into our more complex modern service structure. The fellowship today, composed of members from all over the U.S. and some abroad, was adapted from the simpler service structure our pioneering members established. Those of us working to support the fellowship today are indebted to the effort of these founders, which enabled a much smoother transition. Although Paul stepped away from H.A. World Services in 2012 and passed away sober in 2017, the seeds he and other founders planted are blooming in others' lives today.

As time went on, H.A. began to see meetings spring up all over the U.S. and even in other countries. One early member recalls "groups of groups," calling themselves various service entities (Intergroup, Subdistrict, District, etc.). Groups formed in Texas, California, Pennsylvania, and Ohio early on, followed closely by Alabama, Oregon, Georgia, Colorado, and New York. Like the majority of our fellowship, these groups were mostly started and attended by young people in early sobriety. This brought many new members to H.A., who related to, and felt comfortable in, a fellowship full of younger people.

The troubles of newly formed H.A. groups resulted in many communications to H.A.'s World Services about topics on everything under the sun, from questions about who is really a heroin addict, why certain traditions should not apply, members breaking anonymity, and many more. In some cases, our World Services Board felt crippled: they wanted to help the groups by telling them how to function, but also recognized the need to avoid falling into a management role, which was contradictory to the ideal of the inverted triangle service structure. As a result, the World Services Board recognized the need to unite the fellowship.

This first major effort to unify manifested as a World Convention, occurring in 2014. Nearly two years in the making, the first World Convention was held in Phoenix and hosted many H.A. members from all over the U.S. To date, it remains H.A.'s largest convention, with approximately 1,000 attendees. In addition to being a profoundly significant experience for fellowship, H.A. members from other states could finally converse freely in a way that had not been possible before. An informal network of communication was established among the groups.

In 2015, soon after the first convention, the World Services Board and many of its new friends decided that the next and most important step in uniting the fellowship was to form a World Service Conference. The purpose of the conference was not to fellowship, but rather to have representatives meet for a large business meeting for the overall good of H.A. This would entrust the World Services Board with leadership powers while transitioning primary responsibility to the groups – so the board could better serve them. Thus, the inversion of our triangular service structure was completed. Great efforts were made to have groups elect delegates, and the first H.A. World Service Conference occurred in Portland, Oregon in 2018. It was there that our modern service structure truly began to take shape. The groups' desires, as represented by their delegates, became the spiritual force behind H.A.'s decision-making. Furthermore, the responsibilities of our trusted servants, such as the members of our World Services Board, were clearly delineated. It is this spiritual partnership between the board and the groups that continues today and is responsible for shepherding the groups' vision for a book into a reality.

Gratefully, we recognize that our society was formed by many hands, hearts, and hours of devoted time. We hope that readers will find themselves in these pages – that they too will see their own struggles, hopes, and journeys reflected in the words of those who have walked this path before them. For us here and those to come, may this message be a light in the dark.

WHAT IS HEROIN ANONYMOUS?

Whenever two or more members meet to share their experience, strength, and hope – recovery is possible.

Heroin Anonymous (H.A.) is a fellowship of people whose common purpose is to help others recover from heroin and opioid addiction through the 12 Steps. Our program of recovery was adapted from the program developed by Alcoholics Anonymous (A.A.) in 1935. Although we are not affiliated with A.A., we find that when we apply these 12 Steps to the heroin problem, we can achieve freedom.

By participating in Heroin Anonymous, many individuals have found successful, sustained recovery from heroin and opioid addiction. The program we use allows heroin addicts to better relate, based on each other's experiences.

H.A. continues to attract new members by

adapting our Singleness of Purpose statement to the realities of the spiritual malady. Addiction has not been erased; though heroin is less commonly used in its tar or powder form today, other opioids are still widely available, both on the street and in the pharmacy. Rather than engage in controversial arguments, we focus on what we know. An open mind and a willingness to help others creates unity, not division. Our experience shows that this is beneficial to all of us and ensures our society's survival. Anyone suffering from opioid addiction can benefit from the 12 Steps of Heroin Anonymous, service to others, fellowship with other recovering addicts, and a life committed to spiritual principles.

Today, Heroin Anonymous has continued to evolve in order to reach untold numbers of suffering addicts. For example, ever since H.A.'s early days, some of our members were primarily or solely prescription opioid addicts. Did these members qualify for membership, considering Tradition Three, which originally stated that "The only requirement for H.A. membership is a desire to stop suffering from addiction to heroin"? The differences became less debatable over time as street fentanyl became more prevalent in the mid to late 2010s. While heroin unquestionably still exists, there are now many in our fellowship who are primarily addicted to fentanyl or other opioids. All of these people have a seat in the rooms of Heroin Anonymous.

At its core, H.A. is a set of spiritual principles which can help any willing person achieve freedom from their addiction. When one addict helps another to achieve sobriety, they pass on a message of hope, courage, and love that can save lives. In H.A., we are dedicated to this path. Further, we have found that we have gotten more from the 12 Steps than simple abstinence; our recovery is the foundation of our lives today. We rely on H.A.'s message and fellowship to carry us through the good times and the bad – because it really does work.

WELCOME HOME

Our shared problem and common solution.

Before coming to Heroin Anonymous, many of us attended meetings in other 12-Step fellowships, only to find we didn't quite relate. We frequently focused on how our stories were different because of our heroin use – or worse, we were treated differently because of it. When we talked with others at a 12-Step meeting or group therapy about needles, cotton fever, infection, smoking black tar, and the lengths we went to in order to use, even other addicts sometimes became uncomfortable. This reaction further separated us from the solution that so many of us desperately needed. In many cases, they simply weren't sure how to help, even when they wanted to. The false pride, or inflated shame, we felt still gripped many of us.

For a good number of heroin addicts, endless

doctor and hospital visits became routine. Many of us lived through overdoses, withdrawal sickness, violence, sex work, incarceration, unemployment, the loss of families, and the deaths of those close to us. As you'll read in the personal stories in this book, many heroin addicts were all too familiar with homelessness, panhandling, and theft. We became used to sacrificing our values and sense of self to get high – or just to "get well." The craving and obsession for heroin was so powerful that we often hurt the people who cared for us most, even though we didn't want to. We may have even arrived at a place where we didn't care who we hurt as long as we got what we needed.

We repeatedly faced the judgment, stigma, and pity of the society around us, which didn't grasp our problem – and how could they? Because of the deadly nature of heroin, there existed an increased urgency for heroin addicts to relate to the problem and find a path out. Many heroin and opioid addicts couldn't find the identification and hope they needed until they entered the rooms of H.A. for the first time.

In attending a meeting of Heroin Anonymous, we began to relate. We heard members of the group talk about the marvelous warmth of the first time they used heroin or opioids and how, for many of them, the relief they once felt from heroin almost entirely vanished over time. They said that when they used, their craving was intensified rather than satisfied, and after progressing to a certain point, the desire for a desperate escape was no longer enough to stay stopped. They used *again*. They understood the twin daggers of our addiction: the loss of control when we started to use and the mental obsession to return to heroin after we stopped. For a significant portion of us, all attempts and methods to entirely quit failed miserably. We used heroin when we wanted to, and we used heroin when we didn't want to.

When we finally met other sober heroin addicts who lived our suffering and recovered, we could no longer as easily say, "You don't understand." They knew. They had a way out and were no longer suffering. Just as importantly, they were living life – an idea that seemed impossible for most of us. As the message of recovery was carried to us by another heroin addict, it hit us with a weight we'd never felt before. Regardless of whether the motivation to get sober was driven by our external circumstances or internal pain, we found that when we honestly admitted our problem and became willing to take the 12 Steps, we were on our way. Whether we had lost nearly everything as a result of our addiction or came into the rooms with families and finances intact, we related to our common problem. Later, we would relate to our common solution in our 12 Steps and 24-hour plan for living. Quickly or slowly, we became open to the idea that maybe this could work for us, too. As we recovered, we would experience the same privilege of passing on that very message to the next person in the same way it was freely shared with us. For a great deal of us, the start of recovery began at our first meeting of H.A.

At the heart of Heroin Anonymous is the group. Each H.A. group typically has one or more meetings a week to help the new person find recovery and for sober members to maintain and grow in their sobriety. Most of us choose to make one of these groups our home group, which becomes our anchor to Heroin Anonymous. In our home group, we typically commit to regularly attending and participating in the meetings and find ways to be of service there. The home group is a place where we form lasting relationships and become part of a community in the Heroin Anonymous fellowship.

We discover our family of understanding as hands of friendship are extended to us and we reach out our hand to others. We become helpful, needed, and wanted. We are accepted. For those of us who struggle with the idea of a power greater than ourselves or spirituality, the group becomes a starting place for us to begin to connect in a new way to the world around us. As we continue to participate, we begin to experience freedom from isolation, from ourselves, and others. We feel a real sense of belonging, many of us for the first time. As we go along our way, we may fall short, and our fellows help remind us and uplift us. We, in our turn, look for opportunities to uplift others through both joyous and painful times.

The home group is also a place where we might find a sponsor who guides us through taking the 12 Steps of Heroin Anonymous, which is the core of our program. A sponsor can provide practical suggestions from their experience in the program; they have paved the path for us to recover ourselves. In sponsorship, the majority of H.A. members have utilized the Big Book of Alcoholics Anonymous to take the steps. Helping the next person to achieve sobriety is the lifeblood of our fellowship. Service and sponsoring others are some of the ways we carry our message, and this helps us stay sober ourselves. Frequently, there will be opportunities to carry the message into hospitals and institutions such as treatment centers and correctional facilities. If no such opportunity already exists, we might find ways in our group or community to start. There is no shortage of chances to be of service to other addicts – if we are open and seek them out.

Starting a group or meeting ourselves can be challenging, deeply fulfilling, and rewarding. Many members of H.A. have sat alone in a meeting space, keeping the door open for the new person. We are willing to be available to help others. For those of us starting a meeting, we can be encouraged to know others have laid the tracks. We are not alone in this and can be heartened by the stories of other H.A. members who started groups in their areas. With patience, labor, and love, we can be successful in starting groups ourselves.

It was revealed to us that when we apply the same desperation to the program of Heroin Anonymous as we did to our heroin use, we seldom fail.

We encourage anyone who comes across this book to be honest, open-minded, and willing. We carry faith that we can be uniquely useful to the heroin addict who still suffers, and we hope with God's grace, anyone seeking help with their

addiction can find a solution to their problem
here in Heroin Anonymous.

Welcome home.

Personal Stories

*All of the stories included in the First Edition
of Heroin Anonymous were shared by our
fellowship to help others recover and find
freedom from heroin and opioid addiction.*

THE SECRETS
WE KEEP

*From sex work to international drug use, this
heroin addict didn't expect God would use her wild
experiences to help others find their recovery, too.*

It was 1995, and there I sat next to a penny-
tiled coffee table, gingerly sorting my candy by
color. The tobacco-filled air clouded the meeting
clubhouse where I tagged along with my folks
several times a week. "My name is Joe, and I'm
an alcoholic." "Hi Joe," I echoed from my tiny,
6-year-old frame.

One divorce and two moves later, these 12-
Step meetings were one of the only consistent
parts of my young life. Mom's apartment in a
Southwest city felt empty and dark in comparison.
Bowls of cereal and spilled milk littered the living
room as my brother and I waited for her to wake,
too young to realize that she was drinking again.

I heard from a kid in class that you could kill yourself by cutting your wrists. I went to my Mom for confirmation with superficial scratches on my arms. Within a couple of weeks, I was spending my afternoons with a child psychologist.

I visited Dad at his mountain home during the summer, and he would tell me strange things. I didn't know how strange they were until I was much older. Things like, "I'm not your real Dad." My brother giggled in the front seat of Dad's luxury SUV as this matter-of-fact statement made its way to my ears and knocked the air out of me. That summer, women went in and out of his house like a revolving door. He bought a big motorcycle and would sometimes disappear all night, leaving us with the hired nanny. He often told me, "You have to sleep with a hundred men and sow your wild oats before you're married and it's too late." His 12-Step meetings were a refuge from the chaos and loneliness that waited at home.

Four years later, I gripped the seat of a red hatchback, the sound of my nervous laughter filling the car as my friend whipped his parents' car in donuts around the vacant fairground lot. We were there for the annual meeting round-up, and his rolled cigarette hung from his lips as he turned the wheel with a maniacal smile. He and

I were an unusual pair, bonded by the shared experience of growing up in a 12-Step program. By 15, we were drinking 40 ounces in his hotboxed mobile home, where every rolling tobacco bag he ever bought lined the walls of his bedroom. His home became a meeting place for "black sheep" like me – fellow misfits in our families, churches, and schools. It was a sanctuary of ash-covered floors, graffiti-scrawled furniture, tattooed faces, and pungent-smelling patchwork vests. This was my new safe place. Alcohol flowed and quieted the voice in my head that said, "Smile more, girl," and, "Nobody likes you. They'd all be better off without you." The days and the months passed us by in a daze as we sought a whatever-drug-we-can-get-our-hands-on oblivion. We ditched class, and I soon became a frequent flyer in the juvenile court system. "Do you have any idea what you did last night?" became a familiar refrain.

When I turned 18, I received a court summons for a charge I got as a minor. Dad sat beside me on the hard wooden benches of the courtroom, coaching me on how to get out of this one. "Tell them you have no prior convictions. They can't see that. Tell them you're going to college." I watched others go to the bench and address the judge, but I wasn't worried. I had gotten off easily for drunk driving, possession, public intoxication, and even assault in the past. The bailiff called my name, and I addressed the judge, all confidence and self-righteousness. When the judge asked about priors, I followed Dad's advice. "No, your honor. I've never been in trouble before." She responded, "Young lady, not only do I know that you're lying, but I can see that you appear to have a severe drinking problem."

My stomach dropped to my feet. The judge ordered me to attend substance abuse treatment, but Dad managed to get me out of it somehow, a theme in my troublemaking. "We're not paying $20,000 for you to attend meetings and get a Big Book," he said.

My family decided I would move to Australia for a fresh start, leave "those friends" behind, and get my college degree. In school in Australia, I picked up right where I left off, except worse. The drinking age there was 18, there was a bar in my dorm, and drinking was a huge part of the university culture. Before long, I was failing most of my classes and begging my parents to fly me home.

In the winter of 2010, some friends and I moved into an abandoned house on top of a hill with magnificent views of a nearby harbor in South Australia. The house was formerly a brothel with a red door and a red light out front, which we never changed for some reason. I had six roommates, mostly DJs and folks who sold party drugs. I was the only student, but I didn't fit in at any of the other places I tried living. At one house, I frequently lost my keys and climbed in through the window, or my roommates would find me asleep outside. Once, while tripping on acid, I couldn't figure out how to get inside the house, so I woke everyone up by ringing the doorbell. "Normies" just didn't understand my odd nighttime behavior and my giant pupils.

By then, the 2008 financial crisis had rocked Dad's real estate business, and I had to take financial responsibility for myself and my education. I was working two bartending jobs, going to school, dumpster diving, and living in the squat, but I still wasn't able to make ends meet. I couldn't see that my financial insecurity had everything to do with the fact that I spent all my free time at raves and bars. My entire identity, way of life, and friendships were tied up in acquiring and consuming drugs and alcohol.

I befriended one of the regulars at a pub where I worked. He was an old bloke in his 50s who always kept my favorite pills in his front pocket. He knew about my financial troubles, and one night he joked that he could help me get sorted by putting a mattress in his back room. We could make the money roll in like his ex-wife used to do. A light bulb went on! I already got blackout drunk and disappeared for days at a time, sleeping with God knows who, so I may as well get paid for it. But, I told myself, I'm a college-educated woman of high moral values and a "respectable reputation." His offer was tempting, but I decided I would never be a stripper or a prostitute.

The next day, my new friend connected me with a local biker gang's nude massage parlors, where I was able to start right away. The ladies and I took turns answering the landline phone in the kitchen of a two-bedroom apartment, where the damp mineral smell of baby oil greeted you as soon as you walked through the door. We drank bottles of red wine while waiting for the phone to ring and laughed about the wild and tragic men that came through the door, but the work wasn't always so amusing. The "L" shaped floor plan made the apartment a dangerous trap when a psychotic customer cornered us in a violent rage.

One day, my roommate at the squat was searching for a lighter in my purse and found a stack of cash. "Dude, what are you doing with all this money? Where did this come from?" Secrets poured from me like a kid caught with their hand in the cookie jar. "I do it too," she blurted out. She took me under her wing and introduced me to the world of sex work and hotels, teaching me how to put ads in the paper under fake names, another line in the sand that I quickly and easily leaped over.

Eventually, I moved back home and reconnected with my first love, a wild man I had left behind when I moved to Australia. He welcomed me into his apartment, where I was expecting to party like our old days, but the excitement drained from my body when he told me he was using heroin. I noticed that the room was barren and without furniture, with only a sleeping bag to break up the emptiness. The word "heroin" called to mind old lectures on "hard drugs." I was enraged and disappointed.

My ex switched tack and pulled out a sheet of aluminum foil with a pill. He said it was an oxy, and with little thought, I took the sheet from his hands. After all, pills were safe, familiar, and prescribed by a doctor.

With alcohol, ecstasy, cocaine, and all the rest, I needed a mixture of substances to create the perfect blackout cocktail, something that could erase me as quickly as possible. I used to think I was being roofied at bars until a friend pointed out how quickly I drank. But opiates instantly wrapped me up and numbed the pain that always followed me, the pain of the God-sized hole I didn't even know I had. Now, I could smoke oxy and find oblivion without blacking out and forgetting my name, where my purse was, and whose bed I was in. I immediately had the allergic reaction, or abnormal response, of a drug addict. While my wild man nodded out on heroin, I became hyper. I wanted to smoke those pills all night. When the pills ran out, switching to heroin was just another line in the sand that I danced past. By the next day, we were "flying a sign" at an intersection, maxing out my credit card, and scheming ways to stay high. Within days, I had a needle in my arm.

I would be a slave to heroin for the next six years.

In the end, heroin left me shivering in a hard-plastic chair as I wilted in the overpowered air conditioning of a Southwest detox center with my grandma. Entitlement and self-centeredness dripped off me like poison, and I could feel her frustration and fear. I told her, "I'll do the steps but not the God ones." She said, "You think you're so open-minded, but you're one of the most closed-minded people I know because when I say the word 'God' you shut down." I stared at her with my pink and purple dreadlocks and my sweatshirt pockmarked by cigarette burns. "I'll prove to you there is no God," I thought to myself.

Back at her house, I flipped through a daily reader, and the topic of the day was about sponsorship. It said, "If you don't have a sponsor, pray for a sponsor today." *Okay, challenge accepted.* I made sure the door was locked, the blinds were closed, and a towel was under the door. I got on my knees and said, "Hey, Dude, I don't think you're real, but give me a sponsor or something, thanks." That day, nothing exceptional happened at first. I remember thinking, "So much for God." Grandma took me to a meeting about 40 minutes from her house, but the meeting wasn't there. It had been cancelled. If God cared about me, then "He" would make sure the meeting was there for me, right? A few moments later, another car pulled into the parking lot. A woman stepped out and came over to me as I smoked a cigarette at the back of Grandma's minivan. She said, "Meeting isn't happening? Boy, you look new! Do you need a sponsor?" And that was it. I had my first experience with my Higher Power.

I came to believe that God is the *subject* of an experience, not the *object* of a belief. I ask God for spiritual experiences, and usually I get them. If I am meditating, if I have cleaned house, then I can see and feel spiritual experiences happening all around me.

Recovery didn't happen all at once. About a year later, I was sitting on an old metal chair between my sponsor and a sponsee sibling during a nighttime 12-Step meeting. They didn't know it, but I was using again. The fluorescent lights pierced my mind and body, and I sweated, sniffled, and squirmed as someone read the steps. I thought, "It's only been 20 hours since I last used, my sponsor is letting me sleep on her couch, and no one else cares about me. I cannot mess this up!"

A devil and angel whispered on my shoulder as my insanity grew. I excused myself to the bathroom and pulled out my stashed speedball. Holding it in my hand, I breathed a sigh of relief. I felt like I had finally made the choice to continue forward with recovery. As I returned to the metal folding chair, my heart started pounding. On the drive home, I confessed everything to my sponsor as she understandably expressed her fears and concerns. I had no idea that when I woke up the next morning on her red couch in her boho condo, it would be the first day of the rest of my life. It was January 9, 2014.

I got my six-month key tag at the Living Free meeting of Heroin Anonymous after getting out of a six-month treatment facility specializing in the recovery of sex workers. During this time, I couldn't talk to any men, including the men in my family. This key tag was special. In my disease, I was lonely and isolated. I thought of suicide constantly. So many failed overdose attempts.

Living Free was the first H.A. meeting ever. They met outside near a bonfire pit in the parking lot of a halfway house. In 2014, this meeting was packed with heroin addicts like me who were "doing the deal." The key tag giver called out months, and as the applause grew, my heart was racing again. "Six months?" As I stood up, the sounds of cheers and claps replaced a piece of me that I thought was lost forever in the world I left behind. Their healing hugs pulled me into a realm of love I had not felt in years.

After the meeting, I slid into the driver's seat of my ancient town car and called my little brother to share my excitement. After a few rings, he answered. "Guess what, little bro! I just got my six-month key tag!" He said, "That's great, but how long do you think it will last?" He hung up the phone. I called my sponsor fuming. "How could he do that to me? Doesn't he know what I've been through? The work I've put in?" She calmly replied, "How many times have you lied to him? How many times has it been the last time?" Suddenly, my body felt cold.

It took five years for my brother to trust me. It took about five years for my family to invite me over for the weekend and not just the holidays when everyone is expected to attend. Today, my brother is one of my closest friends.

Living Free and my sponsor propelled me into service work early in sobriety. By 60 days, I was expected to be sponsoring other people. I found that service with the Hospitals and Institutions committee is one of the best ways to get sponsees. My world grew as I joined new committees and got excited about carrying the H.A. message. A friend and I eventually brought the first H.A. meetings into jails and prisons.

Living Free put me in a position to get outside my comfort zone. A group member was on the Heroin Anonymous World Service Board and encouraged me to join when I was two years sober. I was terrified and sat as a silent observer for the first year. I was nominated to be the Chips and Literature chairperson, which grew from a closet in my house to a spare bedroom with a paid employee. My favorite part of the Chips and Literature committee was having access to the official H.A. post office box, which meant answering mail from inmates. There were many days when I sat in my car crying in gratitude for the letters and amends that came to that box.

Still, I sometimes struggled with loneliness in those early years. I found friendly faces and warmth at meetings, but it didn't carry me through once I left the doors of H.A. One day, a firecracker of a lady heard me complaining about this and said, "If you're lonely in H.A., it's your own damn fault because everyone is reaching out their hands to be your friend." I realized that I wasn't reaching out my hand in the way I expected others to do. So, I decided to start new H&I meetings, host fellowship at my house before my home group, and start planning adventures with folks, which turned into an annual trip to Mexico.

In 2016, I was working in a home for girls who all had one thing in common: the Department of Child Safety found their homes and parents unfit for duty. There were 10 girls, ages nine to 17, and their voices echoed through the house as they laughed, fought, and sang. Most of the staff were wonderful but naive interns, and so I was the only one who noticed when a young girl of 15 started coming home with new hair, new nails, a new phone, and a new bag. Acting on instinct, I searched local personal ads online, and there she was – her 15-year-old body on display but her face hidden, only identifiable because of the tattoos her parents gave her. I called the group home manager in a panic and told her, "I think 15 is being sex trafficked."

Together, we were able to shut down a child sex trafficking ring. The pain and suffering that I thought was the most humiliating part of my life helped me recognize the signs of another young person experiencing "the life." God was building me up for that moment, and for every moment when a person walks up to me in the rooms of H.A. and says, "Thank you for being so honest. That's my story too."

In 2017, I married a quirky skateboarder from H.A. who loves the same bad music I do. We got married in my dad's backyard, surrounded by our loved ones. We now have two girls that we get to watch grow up. The other day, my sponsee got her eight-year key tag, and *her* sponsee spoke about how she helped them find God, using the same language that I once heard from my own sponsor.

Today, I write this in absolute gratitude for this program, which gave purpose and meaning to the suffering I endured. If you are new to Heroin Anonymous or recovery, please do not give up. You belong, your story matters, and someone will find healing from the secrets you keep.

A PROBLEM BIGGER THAN HEROIN

*The H.A. program offered relief from a craving
beyond any control this heroin addict could muster.*

It was 9:00 am on a Friday. Not even an hour had passed since I arrived at work, late again. I viciously shivered and shook as the office air conditioning chilled the damp, sweat-stained button-down I'd worn to work every day that week. Every bone in my body ached, and the sharp, jolty spasms and restlessness – one of my least favorite withdrawal symptoms – made it impossible to relax or focus. The only color in my face came from the dark bags under my eyes and the angry scabs where I constantly picked and scratched at my skin. In between yawns, I squinted to see my computer screen. I knew there was a very real possibility that I might throw up or defecate right there in my cubicle. I hadn't slept a minute in nearly three days and hadn't properly rested in months. My anxiety was so strong that suicide was a constant thought. Surely, the only other possible relief from this sickness was the exact substance that caused it. At the time, I believed there was no escape. Everything hurt.

Fridays were typically easy days at the high-end bank where I managed trusts, and my coworkers were all looking forward to the weekend. But I was roughly two days into a heroin kick. If I stuck it out, I knew the weekend would be even worse. I had been on an exceptionally reckless run the past few months, trying to maintain the high that I believed was necessary for me to function well at the bank. This job was fairly new, and it was my first real opportunity after college. I had been so certain that my finance degree and career would be motivation enough to keep me from spiraling, yet here I was, once again desperately covering up my heroin use. I should have known: If life was going good, wouldn't getting high make it even better?

Withdrawal was nothing new, as I'd been through it countless times before, mostly with the help of other narcotics, but the street fentanyl I was detoxing from felt particularly brutal. My mind and body soon entered full panic mode.

Every few minutes, I cycled through an entire spectrum of emotions: doubt, reassurance, pity, anger, and fear. My daily routine at the bank consisted of regular trips to the bathroom to load up small shots that I considered to be my pick-me-ups. They were an effective alternative to morning coffee, lunch, and the other banal activities I saw my coworkers easily enjoy. Lately, I'd been spending additional time in the bathroom puking or sleeping, and although I always found ways to keep my head above water with my responsibilities, I was rarely punctual, often nodded off, and was hardly an ideal employee. On the plus side, I could easily withdraw cash from the ATMs in the bank lobby before sneaking out and rushing across town to score. I thought of each purchase as an investment; I needed it to show up to work at all.

Despite making good money at the bank, on that particular Friday, I didn't have a dollar to my name. I was at the end of the road. In the days prior, I had rear-ended a local police officer during a bout of precipitated withdrawal, checked into my umpteenth treatment center (then left halfway through their intake process), been kicked out of my parents' home again, and gotten my final written warning with the bank. If I took any more time off, I would get fired. Worst of all, I had run out of dope. As the withdrawal gained momentum and my mental status deteriorated, I knew I would have to do what I had done so many times before – give in, find a way to get high, and reevaluate the situation once I could think properly.

Before heroin, I used to have a fairly strong moral compass, established through a typical lower-middle-class upbringing in the South. My parents had me young, were never married, and had been separated my whole life, but they loved me nonetheless. Mom's side of the family was Christian, stable, and extremely involved in my childhood. I was more distant from my dad, who lived a reckless life, a lot like the one I would one day lead. Still, he was there when he could be. I was a social, energetic, curious kid, and always excelled in school and extracurricular activities. When I entered my teenage years, music became a passion, and I developed a drive for creativity and art. Many of the artists I looked up to romanticized drug use, primarily heroin, and in hindsight, I believe a part of me wanted that lifestyle for myself, despite the way I'd been raised.

Alcohol and drugs were common among the kids in my small southern town, and they quickly became my priority in high school. In comparison to a lot of my peers, I began a relationship with opiates at a rather young age and welcomed them into every area of my life almost immediately. I thought they were performance-enhancing drugs; I was at my best on opiates, and I was able to achieve a lot of my successes with their help. At first, I sprinkled heroin with the pills, until the inevitable shift to IV use made me fall in love with "proper" dope. Even as heroin became a bigger part of my life, I thought I still seemed like a socially well-rounded, outgoing, and academically gifted young man. I'm not addicted, I told myself. I'm simply enamored with the feeling and have no interest in living without it. Heroin was my best friend, my therapist, my lover, and my comfort. Naturally, operating while constantly under the influence came with consequences, and in retrospect, no aspect of my heroin use was ever particularly manageable. There were legal, physical, and emotional consequences from the beginning. On the outside, I was a straight-A student, popular athlete and musician, and going to college. Nonetheless, on the inside, I was in constant pursuit of my medicine, no matter the cost – staying well was priority number one.

As I maintained a fairly successful life, my real lifestyle flew under the radar enough to convince me that all the lying, stealing, and dependence on drugs was normal and acceptable. Soon, I was accepted to a state university to pursue a degree in finance. During those four years, I made a notable sum of money working as a musician, which provided steady opportunities and excuses to use the way I wanted to, with little or no questions. I could easily overlook the overdoses, treatment centers, outstanding legal charges, and harm that I was causing. I could overlook the fact that I regularly shot up before exams or stepped away during shows to get high. I missed or slept through classes, and band practice became pointless as I was too loaded to participate, if I even showed up in the first place. As my friends studied and hung out together, I was either going out to score or nodding off alone in my apartment.

My life looked alright from a distance, but up close it was a disaster zone. I was in a cycle of recklessness, selfishness, consequences, fleeting relief, slight successes, and more recklessness. I couldn't see myself for who I really was. Personal, external, and materialistic success were the great delusions that justified my lifestyle.

Naturally, the disease progressed. The high grew harder to achieve and more difficult to maintain. The consequences piled up, and before

I could stop and take an honest look at myself, everything fell apart. My family, who had always tried to help me, was no longer willing to engage in any form of relationship after what I'd put them through. I burned all my social bridges, too – I'd either lied to, stolen from, cheated on, or scarred nearly every person in my life. I had abused every couch I could sleep on, every job I could get, and every opportunity to get help. I was no longer an active participant in my own life, and there was no more external success to hide behind. I lived to use, and chasing the high that I needed left no room for a life outside of heroin. I no longer recognized the person I saw in the mirror. Eventually, loneliness and hopelessness drove me to seek help in a way that I never had before.

Although I'd spent a respectable amount of time in rehabs and detoxes over the years, I had never willingly attended a 12-Step meeting. So, about a year after graduating from college, I walked into my first 12-Step meeting of my own free will, seeking the only type of relief that I knew – instant, short-term, and shallow. It was obvious to everyone there what my drug of choice was, given my appearance, and I was gently pointed to a program specifically dedicated to helping people struggling with heroin addiction.

Although I wanted a new life, I still couldn't picture a future free from heroin, and I believed I just needed to find a way to both get high and maintain a full life. Until I could figure out how to do that, I decided to attend a Heroin Anonymous meeting the following week. Although I did feel a connection with the people in Heroin Anonymous and engaged in the program in my own way, my goals were materialistic and external.

I attended meetings sporadically for what felt like an eternity (nearly half a year of hard-fought abstinence, the longest separation from heroin that I had experienced in as long as I could remember). I learned a lot about what long-term recovery could look like from the people in those meetings, and although I wasn't working the program like them, I managed to actualize many of my goals – a job, a car, and an apartment. This, along with some sleep and a functioning libido, was the only reason I came to H.A. in the first place. I wasn't doing any of the 12- Step work I heard about in the meetings, but I was no longer shooting dope. Therefore, in my mind, I was recovered. Once I was hired in the trust department at a respectable bank, I felt that I had arrived.

Satisfaction followed achievement, and

without any forethought or caution, I celebrated the only way I knew how. This time, it didn't take long for heroin to break me. I was soon facing eviction from the apartment I so desired. Despite all the money I was making and six months of Heroin Anonymous meetings, I was broke and alone.

That's how I found myself detoxing on a Friday morning at work.

As I winced at my desk on that particular day, I knew that I had been through worse kicks, and in worse situations, with worse consequences. The best I could do was use whatever means necessary to get through the detox, which, of course, meant using other narcotics. I managed to tough it out on my own as I'd done before, but remained mentally unwell long after the physical dependence passed.

Based on my history, there was no logical reason to believe that this would be my last withdrawal from heroin, but I was certain that I didn't want to go back. I felt defeated. Of course, that didn't stop me from spending another six months trying to stay clean on my own willpower. At the end of those six months, I was actively suicidal and deeply hopeless. This raised a terrifying question: If heroin was my problem, and

I was now far removed from the heroin problem, then why didn't I feel better? I hadn't been fired. I hadn't lost my home. My external circumstances were as positive as they'd ever been. So, what was wrong with me? Was there no solution to the way I felt without heroin? And how long could I go on feeling like this before using again? These questions, and the lack of answers, put me in the worst depression I had ever experienced. I was lost, alone, hopeless – and entirely sober.

During this depression, I reflected on what I heard at Heroin Anonymous meetings. I remembered people who used the same way I did, yet found a way to stay clean, and more importantly, who seemed happy, as if they were somehow both clean from heroin and enjoying their lives. This was the great mystery, and the main reason I came back to the same Tuesday night H.A. meeting after so long away. I came back to the program hollow, scared, and spiritually broken. I was willing to try anything to stop feeling the way I felt. I knew that regardless of my situation, I would eventually either get high, as I'd always done, or commit suicide. I now knew I was suffering from a very real problem – a problem that existed even without heroin, and a problem that I was incapable of solving alone. I was willing to place my dependence on the program. I didn't know that attending that Tuesday night H.A. meeting would completely change my life.

The welcome I received upon my return was completely disarming. The acceptance I was shown, not in spite of my relapse but because of it, lessened the self-pity and remorse I carried in with me. Although it felt unnatural, I accepted their welcome and friendship. I quickly inserted myself into the group and took the suggestions they offered me. Life became a whirlwind of handshakes, phone numbers, and invitations to fellowship. That night, I felt like I wasn't alone for the first time in years; I truly related to these people. I knew that they saw me, heard me, and understood me. It was as if I had done exactly what I was supposed to do, and was now exactly where I was supposed to be. I saw why those people stuck together.

In the past, I came in intending to do things *my* way, despite having years of experience that showed me where my way would take me. This time, out of fear, I consciously chose to avoid judgment and say yes to the suggestions laid out by the men and women trying to help me. I decided I would give the program an honest try, and if it didn't work, I would go back to living my life as best I could. I am endlessly grateful that since working the Twelve Steps as outlined in the Big Book of Alcoholics Anonymous, I have not yet felt it necessary to go back to my old way of living. Moreover, the desire to use heroin has been removed in its entirety. I have been given a way of life that allows me a freedom that I have never experienced before.

I learned I had been living with a physical reaction to heroin that creates within me a craving beyond any control I can muster. I had also been trying to operate with a mind that continuously brought me back to getting high, whether I wanted to or not. The physical and mental aspect of my addiction was compounded by a total lack of belief in anything other than myself. I thought I chose the life I lived, I got myself into the situations I was in, and I would get myself out of them on my own. When dependence on myself failed me for the last time, the hopelessness of my condition became unbearable. Yet, I still didn't want to stop using or do any work to change my life, and I certainly did not want to believe in anything other than myself.

When I look back on the time leading up to my return to Heroin Anonymous, I believe it was necessary for me to lose faith in myself to become willing to place my dependence on something greater. Against my own plans and designs, that last relapse granted me the willingness to change. The help I received in Heroin Anonymous has allowed me to amend and restore my relationships. I can actively participate in my own life again. I am no longer alone. I have found true freedom and connection through working the Twelve Steps in the program of Heroin Anonymous.

The effect that heroin gave me was profound. In order to successfully stay away from heroin, I needed a solution that was equally, if not more, profound. The program of Heroin Anonymous has given me that beyond anything I could have imagined. In my most desperate and most hopeless state, I found the ultimate solution in the rooms of H.A.

HAPPY FOR FREE

*An FDA-approved opioid medication opened
the door to years of suffering. Spirituality
helped this addict find a way out.*

When I first entered the rooms of Heroin Anonymous, I just wanted to end the daily dope-sickness. I had no idea I was beginning a process of transformation that would result in me becoming the best version of myself. This process continues to work in my life, helping me rise above the shortcomings that are innate to the human condition.

Unlike some people, I can't trace my heroin habit back to my childhood. My upbringing was happy and stable. My parents only drank occasionally, and out of my hundreds of relatives, only three of us became addicts or alcoholics, so I can't cite a genetic or environmental reason that explains my heroin addiction. My teenage years had me smoking weed regularly and drinking on the weekends but still performing well in my responsibilities. If you had lined me up with my friends in those years, you would never have picked me out as the one who would end up in the rooms of Heroin Anonymous. But outward appearances are not inward reality, and a spiritual malady would form when I was 20 years old. A devastating event occurred in my life, and I suffered a deep wound to my spirit that no human means could resolve.

My addiction to opioids began in 2003 when a new "non addictive" opioid medication was just beginning its path of destruction across the country. This FDA-approved medication would change an entire generation forever. A friend offered me one of those little blue pills late one night, and a rush of joy and serenity entered my soul. I had used plenty of other drugs recreationally, and I had no reason to think this one would be any different. I decided that I would add this drug to my normal routine, but just on the weekends, as I had responsibilities, of course. I had begun a process of justification and rationalization that resulted in an endless supply of "good" reasons why "right now" was never the time to stop. All my attempts to regulate my use failed.

The process of addiction continued for several years, a habit formed, and my daily quota for opioids became more expensive. I honestly don't know how I was able to maintain my habit for so long. In 2005, my family sent me to Europe for a month. That sounds awesome, unless you're strung out. I couldn't decline the offer, as that would have raised many pointed questions. I just had to figure out how to stay well while thousands of miles from my dealer. So, I came up with a plan. I realized that if I took a little piece of a pill each day for 30 days, I wouldn't get sick – I had figured it out! I proudly departed for Europe with this foolproof plan. A week later, I was completely out and dopesick. I had no prospects or plans on how to resolve the crisis. My great plan didn't factor in the most important piece of information: I am a heroin addict. As a heroin addict, the time to use is always "right now." The flimsiest excuse became a reason to use more. My plan to control my use resulted in crisis and withdrawal.

Upon returning from Europe, I decided that I couldn't go on... affording my habit. I still liked the getting high part, so I began taking a new medication that was used by many addicts to taper off their use. I figured I would taper off over 90 days. Two and a half years later, I was still on the same dose because it was never the "right time" to taper. I was still dependent on a chemical; only my living conditions had stabilized. For reasons I cannot explain, I made the worst decision of my life – I went cold turkey while on the maximum dose of this medication. I had no idea what I had just begun. After a few of the worst days of my life, I believed that, surely, there could only be a few more days left of this hell before I was out the other side. If someone had told me on day three that I would have *30 more days* of gut-wrenching detox, I would have tapped out right then, but I kept on believing that I only had a few more days to go. No normal person would put themselves in that position *again*. But I'm a heroin addict, and with the mind of a heroin addict, that's exactly what happened. A seemingly trivial excuse presented itself seven months later. I had found some professional success once I was freed of my physical dependency and was due to go on an annual camping trip. Prior to leaving, the idea came to me that this trip was a special occasion, and I could pick up some pills to celebrate. Just one time wouldn't physically addict me – that's science! So, I picked up, used, and wasn't sick the next day. I had figured it out! Just on the weekends, that was the key!

Once my mind found that these excuses worked, it manufactured many more in rapid succession. Soon, "Tuesday" was a great excuse to get high. So began a run that would last twice as long as my first one and progress from pills to heroin. If you had asked me during those years if I was going to stop, I would have exclaimed, "Yes! By my next birthday, for sure." This thinking let me defer responsibility for getting sober while still feeling like I was doing something about it. This continued for seven years, but it wasn't seven years in the conventional sense. It was seven years of the same day over and over again. My attempt to dictate the course of my addiction had failed.

My heroin addiction didn't necessarily take my soul all at once, but in a series of small pieces and concessions. It was an abusive relationship; I abused heroin, and it abused me. Heroin started by demanding my time, so I gave it away. Then, heroin asked for my property, so I turned it over. Finally, heroin asked for the sanity of my family, so I sacrificed it on the altar of my addiction. I wouldn't have rent money, so I would ask my family for help (with an extra hundred dollars on top to get well, of course), and at the same time feel proud of myself for not asking my family to finance my addiction. Only later, when I asked myself why I didn't have rent money in the first place, did I realize that my family was financing my addiction all along. Even my girlfriend began engaging in sex work to finance our addiction, and I looked the other way because I didn't want anything to interrupt the flow of heroin money. I became a parasite.

I didn't know it, but a profound change was on the horizon. I had no idea I was on the verge of passing into a life so beautiful that I can barely describe it with words.

At 32 years old, I was on a mattress on a floor facing another eviction, and I was talking to my sister when she offered to try and help with my addiction. I accepted, but I wanted to find help that was not 12-Step based, as I believed it was a brainwashing scheme. However, I soon learned about the existence of Heroin Anonymous. At that time, I was totally unable to listen to anyone who wasn't a heroin addict like me. I still believe there is something special about one opioid addict working with another that can't be perfectly replicated elsewhere.

I met people in Heroin Anonymous who used just like I did, many of them much worse, and they found a way to be sober and happy at the same time. When I began working the steps, I started from a place of total defeat in my decision-making process, so I just listened and worked. I didn't have any fight in me to question things any longer. I just didn't want to be dopesick anymore, and if doing the steps would get me well, then I was more than willing to do them. If my dealer told me he would take away my dopesickness if I wrote out some resentments, I would have eagerly grabbed the pen and gotten to work. I took that same belief and dove into my step work. The steps have this in common with heroin: You can only truly understand them by doing them.

A crucial part of the 12-Step process is making amends. I was tempted to try and begin making amends well before it was the proper time to do so. Those amends would have been selfish because I was only making them to relieve my guilt rather than amending a behavior that caused harm. I was told that the steps are in order for a reason and rushing the process would only lead to more harm. I'm glad I listened. There are few situations in life more humbling than making an amends purely for the sake of making amends, with no expectations.

When I was four months sober, I felt it was time to make amends to my mother's friend, who I owed money. I called him and explained my recovery and asked if he would be willing to hear my amends. He agreed to meet me. I knew I couldn't make amends to this man without a payment, so I gave him $40, which was almost all I had to my name. A few days later, I was offered a job that I hadn't even applied for! God provides when we do the work. I continued making payments until I repaid all the money I owed. This man died several months later, and I realized I had made amends to this man in the last months of his life and didn't even know it. This taught me that if I am in the right place in my steps and I feel my Higher Power wants me to make amends, I don't make excuses – I make appointments. Some amends are easy, and others can be scary, but each one is beautiful in its own right.

Service work also took center stage in my recovery. I attended an H.A. meeting on Friday nights, and within weeks, I was a home group member picking up cigarette butts and trash after the meeting. How many people can say that picking up cigarette butts changed their life? In my case, it couldn't be more true. I felt a satisfaction from being helpful that was totally alien to me. In fact, I had found a new high: being of service. Like many people in early sobriety, the fellowship of H.A. and my many service commitments became my whole world. I may have taken this commitment to an unhealthy level, but what can you expect from a heroin addict? A friend reminded me, "If you're going to practice the principles in all your affairs, you need other affairs." I took his advice to heart and began redirecting my passion inward and bringing balance to my life. This process of self-evaluation and spiritual guidance is never complete; it is ongoing, but that is actually good, because that means I continue to grow as a person. We strive for spiritual growth rather than spiritual perfection.

At the core of the whole process is making a connection to a power greater than myself, the side effect of which is that I don't obsess about using heroin today. I must treat my spiritual sickness daily through meditation, prayer, and service. If I fail to take my "spiritual medicine," then my malady acts up and the obsession returns. When this happens, my choices are either to devote myself back to the spiritual program of H.A. or to use again and set the cycle back in motion. Fortunately for me, my near misses have resulted in getting grounded in recovery again. I take comfort in the promise that I can be both sober and happy at the same time.

Heroin Anonymous saved my life when no

other force on earth could. I found fellowship, purpose, and a God of my understanding. Today, I appreciate things big and small, I have a guide for living that works, and a moral code to live by. When I reflect on my life, I am even grateful for my time in active addiction before I became a member of Heroin Anonymous because there was purpose in my suffering. I am grateful that my life got so bad that I was forced to begin a process that brought me closer to the Spirit of the Universe. Being human, I still have my problems, but when it comes to my heroin addiction, there is no more suffering.

WAKING UP

*Admitted to treatment with absolutely nothing,
this addict found help, acceptance, and hope
in the rooms of Heroin Anonymous.*

I came to, confused and disoriented. My older sister stood over me with eyes full of tears. She shouted my name. I slowly looked around the room, willing my memory to return. My sister had agreed to let me stay with her for a little while so I could get my life back on track. She always looked out for me and was one of the only people I had left who hadn't written me off as hopeless. I hadn't been out of treatment for more than 48 hours. As I sat up, a syringe slid out of my arm and landed on the floor. I saw the burnt spoon next to it.

My next memories are mostly a blur, but I vividly recall walking down the road with her slowly shadowing me in her car – crying, screaming, begging me to return. I couldn't. I just wanted to get high. I yelled back to her, "I'm fine," over and over. The next thing I remember: sitting in a packed parking lot trying to decide what my next move should be. I'd been spending a lot of time sitting in parking lots. The heat from the pavement helped lessen the withdrawals. I wondered if this was a dream.

I spent the next several years as a nomadic drug fiend, desperately digging through my past life to find any long-lost friends who could give me a place to sleep for a few nights and, if I was lucky, lend me a small amount of money. Somehow, I ended up in California, staying with a friend and his wife, but the friendship came to an abrupt end. My mind was still focused on one thing: getting high. I stayed in California for a couple more years, imagining all the while how my life could be different, only to wake up each day to find life exactly the same as the day before. I was in the sunniest city in the most populated state, but I felt darker and more alone than ever.

I planned on taking my life then. The eternal sleep. Taking the "easy" way out. However, there was nothing easy about it. Deep down within myself, I knew I didn't deserve anything remotely easy. I deserved consequences and punishment for all the horrible things I said and did to the people who loved me the most. I deserved to live this way, tired and scared. No California dreamin' for me.

When I moved back to my home state, I was immediately arrested on a bench warrant. I had genuinely lost track of any active warrants at this point. I had a practiced performance for each judge I stood before, full of tears and empty promises. I guess I had gotten pretty good at the routine because I was, once again, released on my own recognizance. By chance, I had the opportunity to speak with my brother, who was getting processed at the same time I was being released. We had been through so much together, and it was good to know he was still alive, even if his arms were covered in bruises and he looked like death. I'm sure I looked identical.

I walked out of the courthouse with no money and no place to go. I found myself sleeping on a bench in an isolated park, eating scraps of food out of dumpsters. By day, I discreetly charged my ankle monitor at the local businesses that hadn't banned me yet. I spent most of my nights reminiscing on how I got here, where I went wrong, and asking myself, "Why me?" I knew I was broken beyond repair.

I hit another bottom when I snuck into a friend's house through his doggy door. I wasn't even looking for drugs or money. I just wanted to get out of the endless rain and cold for a moment.

That moment led me to a half-hearted desire to go back to rehab, not because I actually thought it could help, but because I desperately needed a bed and some food, even if only for a few days. I pleaded with strangers to let me use their phones, calling the treatment centers I'd written down on a crumpled piece of paper. Once they heard I had no insurance and no means to pay, they politely rejected me. Eventually, I got lucky and found a treatment center that was willing to scholarship me.

I never had any hope it would be different this time, so I hid a syringe outside the facility. It was so dull from overuse that it probably couldn't even be considered a syringe anymore. The analogy wasn't lost on me. I was admitted with nothing. No money. No personal belongings. Not even hope. Or so I thought. A part of me had finally found some willingness. A willingness to take suggestions. A willingness for something new. What should have been five days turned into a month, and the staff suggested that I go to a halfway house after my discharge. Despite the horror stories I'd heard about these places, I agreed. The only realistic alternative was going back to a sad and lonely park bench.

Checking into the halfway house, I was hit with a lengthy list of rules. They said I couldn't do drugs anymore, I had to get a job, I had to pay rent, finish all my chores, attend a meeting every day, get a home group, find a sponsor and call them once a day, and work the Twelve Steps. So that's exactly what I set out to do. This is when and where I found my first Heroin Anonymous meeting. It was filled with people who looked like me and had similar stories to mine... except they weren't me. They were happy. I wasn't. I was extremely curious how they had accomplished this miracle.

This became my first home group in Heroin Anonymous. I was given a service commitment, I asked someone to sponsor me, and I began the Twelve Steps shortly after. The journey from this point is unique to each individual. For me, I quietly began to wake up, spiritually. I never had to pick up that syringe I hid outside that treatment center. I uncovered my character defects and my core fears. I made my amends and completed my restitution. I rekindled broken relationships while making new and lasting ones. I reinvested in my education and became gainfully employed. I have a warm and loving home that I can call my own, along with a beautiful and supportive partner by my side.

I learned that recovery doesn't mean I'm immune from making mistakes, experiencing mental health struggles, or even facing tragedy and loss. I've encountered all of these in my recovery. Even sober, I've caused harm, lost employment, lost material possessions, and ended relationships. I've lost a lot of friends along the way and even some family, including that same brother I miraculously crossed paths with at the courthouse. He died from an overdose years later, alone in his room. Life was providing plenty of struggles, and yet I was facing them. Heroin Anonymous helped me overcome the overwhelming and grow from each experience. I'm truly grateful I have a fellowship around me and support when I need it most.

So, I continue to rely on what got me here – the suggestion to get a sponsor, the suggestion to work the steps, the suggestion to attend meetings, the suggestion to get a home group, the suggestion to get a service commitment, and the suggestion to help those who are still struggling with their addiction. I depend on the people I've met in

Heroin Anonymous for guidance, friendship, and accountability. I rely on the newcomer to remind me where I come from. Maybe someone else's brother will have the chance to call me if they find themselves alone and needing help.

Today, I've finally found myself. I see a new me in the mirror. I've found my happiness, and I'm not alone anymore. My eyes are wide open, and I get to experience the beauty and, yes, the misery of the world all around me. Now, I can face it. Heroin Anonymous has given me all this and more.

I DIDN'T THINK IT WOULD BE A PROBLEM

This fentanyl user found that his "perfect" sponsor was the one who carried the message of recovery.

My story starts in the 1990s, with a family of four in Southern California. My parents always told me they wanted one boy and one girl. They got their wish – me, the youngest, towhead blond boy, and my sister, just two years older. My parents always taught me right from wrong. Don't drink, don't do drugs, go to church, and so on. They never drank or used drugs during my entire childhood, but some other family members did. I watched my grandparents and sister go in and out of the rooms and treatment for years on end. I wondered why they couldn't get a hold of themselves. At a family gathering one day, I believe I was about nine years old, I snatched my grandmother's full glass of wine and completely finished it in a matter of seconds. I think I did it for the shock value. She simply laughed and said, "Don't tell anyone." During my younger years, that's how I used – to get attention. I never thought for a second it would become a problem.

Years went by and the fun continued. By age 20 I had lost control of the amount I was drinking. I began to make attempts at moderating and controlling my use. I bought bottles that I planned to last a week, and they would be gone in hours. Once I could buy alcohol legally, I gave up on moderation. I drank as much as I could, and I soon went in search of substances that could help me drink longer and harder. Stimulants like methamphetamine and cocaine became a weekend ritual, and eventually a daily routine. I found that I could drink all day long, at work, at home, and with friends, so long as I kept a pipe on me.

I spent years working construction jobs I hated, always finding refuge in my pipe. Slowly, my meth use became more important than the alcohol. Nights and days became weeks without sleep. I could not hold myself together. I could not drink myself to sleep. So, I set out on my next stage of development. A search to modify the chemical cocktail recipe I had spent so long perfecting. I wondered what could help me come down from these stimulants successfully?

I soon got into a relationship with another guy, and it was a match made in heaven; me, the alcoholic tweaker, him a recovering opioid addict. I met him with absolutely zero knowledge of what it took to be sober. I knew he had been in rehab the year prior and was currently prescribed a medication to deal with his opioid addiction. It never crossed my mind that we probably shouldn't be drinking together. Meanwhile, I was twisting the pipe in private, until one day he caught me, and so naturally we started doing it together. We fell into a drug-induced love.

A day came when his medication ran out and he had no insurance or ability to obtain any more. He explained that he was going to get sick, and it wouldn't be pretty. I didn't understand what was in store. I had never seen anything like it. He was vomiting, screaming, shaking, sweating. I thought he was going to die. I held him as long as I could, and he finally broke down and told me the only way to help him would be to get him heroin. And so I did.

I had watched him in such extreme agony for over a week that it was not a hard choice to make. I thought I was doing the right thing. He told me where to go, how much money to bring, and what kind of paraphernalia to get. I quickly rushed home with everything he had requested. And when I watched him go from death's door to being able to run a marathon in a matter of seconds, I knew I had to try this miracle drug.

Opioids changed me. To this day it is hard to find the words to articulate how. Their hold on me was immediate. These drugs gave me everything I ever wanted. I felt I had finally perfected the recipe to my drug cocktail, but this success was short-lived. I soon found myself choosing drugs over everything. Giving up multiple homes, losing cars, and disregarding family and friends soon became normal to me. Going in and out of detox centers became a monthly affair.

An entire decade passed in a daze. I finally woke up inside the county jail. I'd never been in trouble with the law before, and all of a sudden, I was facing multiple felony drug sales charges. The moment I was released, I was loaded again.

After another year or so of chasing the high, I was now smoking all the fentanyl I could get my hands on. By then, heroin had disappeared, and the fentanyl high was so short that I had to spend my entire day searching for it. It was draining. I went days without food, living out of stolen cars, often telling myself, "I've had enough of this." One day I was parked in a parking lot when I decided to make a last-ditch effort and call my mother for help. Like any good junkie, I put just enough hunger and helplessness into my voice. She agreed to take me to a detox facility I had been to a few times, but the next thing I knew a cop was knocking on my window. He had arrested me before. He asked me to get out of the vehicle and if I remembered him. I rolled my eyes. "Of course I do," I said. As he searched my car, I promised him he wouldn't find anything. I had been sitting in that car for days, dopesick and hoping to die. Every speck was gone, every baggie was licked, and every pipe and stem was scraped. "What is this?" he asked. Against all odds, he found something I'd missed. I was so upset – upset that I hadn't found it and smoked it sooner. He told me he was going to take me in because of what he found, and then he mentioned I also had a bench warrant. Here we go again.

I quickly explained to him that my family was on their way to take me to detox. I pleaded with him and told him (like any good junkie) I was done and really wanted to stop this time. That was a lie; I had no intention of stopping. I wanted to grab that sack out of his hand and run. That day he showed me grace, and when my mom arrived, he let me go to treatment instead of jail.

A week later it was my birthday, and I remember I spent it on the floor of the detox bathroom, shaking and trying to keep my body close to the cold floor as I experienced withdrawal. I was going in and out of psychosis from lack of sleep, and I remember peeing my pants, wondering if I was hallucinating, and all the while saying to myself, "Happy 30th birthday." The treatment center took me to court, where I asked to be placed in a 90-day county program to avoid jail time. They agreed. They sent me to a facility that encourages 12-Step work on a county bed scholarship.

I entered this program unwillingly, like all the others. If I had my way, I would have been in a motel room watching crappy reality TV with enough heroin and meth to last me for weeks. The staff told me to get a sponsor, attend all programming throughout the day, and work the steps. I had never thought about working the Twelve Steps before I entered this treatment center. I had only been to one meeting in my life, and only to meet another drug addict and pick up drugs. I thought to myself, if I am going to stay here, I may as well put my all into it and see what comes of it. My peers told me I would be able to pick my own sponsor and that there were a lot of alumni from the facility who came back around to help take us through the Twelve Steps. I thought this would give me some time, and I started dreaming up the perfect sponsor. That soon ended when a guy came up to me and told me he was going to be my sponsor. I was confused. He was nothing like the person I had been picturing, but before I knew it, he promised to come back the next day to get me started on my steps.

We sat down the next day to get to know each other. He was the complete opposite of me. Different race, sexuality, religion, drug of choice – nothing added up. He was eight years younger than me. "Still a child!" I thought. What was this guy going to do for me? He hadn't even been sober for more than five months! We began to read the book *Alcoholics Anonymous*. He started breaking it down for me, answering my questions, and pointing out important parts of the book. He started off by reading, "We, of Alcoholics Anonymous, are more than one hundred men and women who have recovered from a seemingly hopeless state of mind and body." I was stunned, and suddenly overwhelmed with a feeling of comfort. This was the first time I truly felt there might be a way out, a way to wake up without the overwhelming need to get loaded, a way to live life without suicidal ideation, a way to get my life back.

In the following days, I kept hearing a lot of the same words. Words to do with honesty, open-mindedness, and willingness. I was told that if I worked all Twelve Steps, a spiritual experience would occur that would lead to a drastic shift in the way I view life, something they called a "psychic change." I thought these guys were weird. I didn't know what that meant, but I set out on the course of action they described because I wanted what they had. I got to work, and I kept reading the Big Book.

By the end of my 90 days in the facility, I had finished my Step work, and my sponsor explained to me that when I left it would be vital to practice Steps 10, 11, and 12 daily. He said the process of taking inventory, along with prayer, meditation, and sponsoring others, would be the means to maintain permanent sobriety. He explained to me the promises of the Big Book, that if I kept close to God and did His work well, my drug problem would be removed. He said I would be safe and protected. He said that it wouldn't even be a struggle, and that it would happen automatically. I have found that all of these promises have come true, which is why I continue to work this program to this day. Taking others through the Twelve Steps is now one of the brightest spots of my life. I quickly met a group of addicts through Heroin Anonymous who enjoyed recovery and the Twelve Steps as much as I did. I have been a member of H.A. for years now. Attending H.A. weekly, sponsoring people, and being a part of this fellowship have brought me closer to God, my fellows, and given me an amazing group of misfits in my life that I am proud to call my friends.

I worked the Twelve Steps, and by the grace of God, I recovered. I continue to work these Twelve Steps, and I stay recovered. The promises came true. I have been able to maintain sobriety even while ending that long, drug-induced relationship, as well as the loss of family and friends. I have even implemented the solution I found in the Twelve Steps in other areas of my life. God removed the obsession to use drugs and alcohol, so why not access this Power in other parts of my life? By turning over my career, dating, education, family, and relationships to God, they have all become exponentially more beautiful. By practicing these principles, they have strengthened my relationship with all of my family members in ways I never could have dreamed.

I now realize this Power has always been there; I just didn't know how to access it. I never cared to look. It took years of active addiction to compel me to search for it. And today, I am extremely grateful for those years. I cherish this new way of life like a gift. I have recovered. It is not because of something I did. It has been God's plan all along. Today, I know that the cop letting me go that day in the parking lot was not luck; it was God. It was a Power greater than myself acting in my life without my permission. God kept me alive through my active use, placed me into that treatment center, and introduced me to Heroin Anonymous and this design for living, and I will forever be in debt to the program of Heroin Anonymous. The Twelve Steps have given me freedom that I never thought possible.

ENOUGH

*Getting high against her will forced this heroin
addict to find a solution to her powerlessness.*

All I ever wanted was to be enough. Enough
for myself. Enough for others. To this day, I don't
know why I felt that way – no one ever told me I
wasn't good enough – but I felt the ache of being
less than every day. Of being a disappointment.
In fact, if I think about it, my whole life has been
shot through with that single word – enough.

I was always looking at the people around
me and wondering, how can I be like them? How
can I be loved and accepted? As if life was a math
equation, and if I could just solve for x, then I
would find the happiness that always seemed to
elude me. I tried anything I thought would make
a difference. I was sure that if I had the right hair,
clothes, friends, or boyfriend, then I would be
happy.

Eventually, my attempts to be someone else led me to hanging out with a crowd of people who were into partying, which led me to the moment I tried alcohol for the first time. Drunk at a party, I found myself looking around at these people I had admired so much. They were still pretty, funny, smart, and lovable, but for the first time in my life, I felt like I was too. In fact, I couldn't remember why I ever felt like I wasn't. For a few hours that night, I found what I had always been looking for. I was enough.

I woke up the next morning full of anticipation for what my life would be like now that I was this changed person. I went to school ready for the first day of the rest of my life, but when I got inside, I found that all of my fears and insecurities were still there. I was crushed. Where was the girl who felt so sure of herself? Where was the girl who finally felt like she was worthy of love?

The next weekend I found myself at another party, and I wondered: What would happen if I had a beer? So, I drank a beer, and then I drank another, and a short while later, I found myself once again feeling like I belonged. Alcohol gave me a reprieve from my fears, and I began to look forward to those days and hours when I could drink away all those feelings of being less than.

I thought I had found my solution, but what I actually found was that my relationship with that word "enough" was changing. Now, instead of obsessing over *being* enough, I began to obsess over *having* enough. I was no longer satisfied with a few hours of happiness on a Saturday night; I wanted to feel this way all the time. The amount I drank increased too, because surely if two beers made me feel happy, then three beers would make me feel even happier. And what about four or five? The limit to how far I was willing to go to escape myself didn't seem to exist.

I began to experiment with other drugs like marijuana and cocaine. Really, I was willing to try anything I was offered. My threshold for pain was dropping rapidly, and the hours that I wasn't high were becoming intolerable. Then, one fateful day, I was offered a piece of tin foil with heroin on it, and my answer, of course, was yes.

It's hard to explain what heroin did for me. If alcohol made my problems feel small, then heroin made me forget I had problems to begin with. From that moment on, I used heroin every chance I got. When the opportunity wasn't there, I made the opportunity. When I didn't have money to buy it, I sold my stuff. When I was out of things to sell,

I stole. The only thing I was sure about anymore was that I needed to be high, consequences be damned. And there were consequences.

I have a brother who is 10 years younger than me, and he is my favorite person in the world. He always has been, since the day he was born. Being the older sister, I took care of him a lot, and to say I would do anything to protect him is an understatement. I love him fiercely and would do anything to keep him from getting hurt, or, at least, I liked to think I would.

On the day of his eighth birthday, I snuck into my parents' room and stole his present out of their closet. I took it to the pawn shop, used the money to buy dope, and showed up late and high to dinner that night. When I sat down, he was talking to my parents about all of the things he had done to deserve a present, clearly trying to understand why he hadn't gotten one. My parents tried to make excuses for why they didn't have a gift to give him – it was just lost in the mail – but he didn't understand. All he knew was that for some reason he didn't get a present for his birthday. For some reason, he wasn't good enough.

All I wanted at that moment was to tell them what I did. All I wanted was to tell him that of course he deserved a birthday present. But I couldn't. The feeling of not being good enough was so intolerable to me that I was willing to shoot poison into my veins to avoid it, but in that moment, I let the person I loved most in the world suffer with that feeling so that I didn't have to. I let him experience all of that pain so that I could walk out of there that night and get high again, and I had never hated myself more.

The consequences got worse from there, technically, but I had never felt worse. A trip to jail was nothing compared to the feeling of hurting the people you love the most. If guilt and shame were enough, I would have gotten sober that day, but I didn't.

I began to cycle in and out of rehab and was eventually sent to a halfway house. They told me I had to go to a 12-Step meeting every day, get a sponsor, and work the steps. I didn't really know what that meant, and I didn't really know how it would help. I went through the motions, but I never really tried. Unsurprisingly, I couldn't stay sober.

Then, something happened. I had just gotten out of jail and gotten back to the rundown, cockroach-infested apartment where I was living with my best friend. I was dopesick and had a shot ready in my hand... and tears started to fill my eyes. I wanted to feel better so badly, and yet I knew that I wouldn't. My friend told me that if I didn't want to get high, then I should just... not get high. I couldn't understand. I didn't want to do it, but I knew that I would. How could I not?

That day, I finally understood what it meant to be powerless. In my previous attempts at sobriety, I had been asked if I believed that I was powerless, and I always said yes. I would say I was powerless because I couldn't hold a job. Because my car was impounded. Because my family wouldn't speak to me. But on that day, I finally realized that wasn't true at all. None of those things made me powerless. I was powerless because no matter what, left to my own devices, I would get high again. The realization was terrifying.

I packed the few things I owned and checked back into the halfway house I had been living at before. They told me I had to go to a 12-Step meeting every day, get a sponsor, and work my steps just like before. But this time, I worked like my life depended on it. Unsurprisingly, this time, it worked.

Through working the steps, I learned about the behaviors and fears that led me to use in the first place. And I also learned that just learning about those things meant nothing. I had to take action to change those behaviors or I would get high again. Most importantly, I learned that I needed help. It takes immense faith to face your fears, and the purpose of the Big Book is exactly that – to connect you to something, anything, that you can put your faith in to get you through the change. With faith, I can finally be enough.

The result is that I have stayed sober for 13 years and counting. Thirteen beautiful, amazing, hard, challenging, rewarding years. I have been given the tools to deal with life exactly as it is and to deal with my feelings exactly as they are. I have learned that I'm lovable and worthy and, most importantly, that I am more than enough. I know that deep in my heart today, and I don't need a drink or a drug to feel it. On days that I don't feel that way – and there are days that I don't – I have a community of people to lean on and help me through. I haven't been alone for a single day since I got sober, and as the promises tell me, I never have to be alone again.

And for that, I am grateful.

A JOURNEY FROM DESPERATION TO HOPE

*Chronically depressed, suicidal, and sick, this
addict found God through acts of service.*

I first tried heroin when I was 18, but my
using career really started when I was 12 or 13.
It began with alcohol and just kind of escalated
from there. Some pretty horrific things happened
after I discovered heroin – I gave up a child for
adoption and lost custody of another. I watched
people die from this disease right in front of me.
Things got so bad that my family wouldn't see
me anymore. I was homeless in a large city in the
Southwest, bouncing around from place to place,
and I had some serious medical issues that landed
me in the hospital more than once. Eventually, I
ended up in jail.

I knew my life was out of control when
heroin – a downer – became necessary just for

me to get up and function. I couldn't do anything without heroin, and even when I had it, I needed to pile on more substances just to feel okay. The lowest, rock-bottom point of my addiction is hard to pinpoint. Was it when I was homeless? In jail? Sitting in a courtroom crying as I signed away my rights to my child? It could have been any of those moments. During those dark times, I thought about death a lot. I would write suicide notes, find them weeks later, and get upset that I was still alive – then write new ones to try again. I'd wake up angry that the drugs hadn't killed me in my sleep. Every day felt like another failed escape attempt. Eventually, the way I was surviving caught up to me and I ended up in prison. This was a surprise to no one, especially considering that I'd been arrested 17 times in seven months in 2012 alone.

When I got out of prison, I had nowhere else to go, so I checked into a sober living house. The day I arrived, I went to my first 12-Step meeting, and it was a spirituality topic meeting. I walked into the room and realized I was the youngest person there by about 30 years. Everyone was over 50, and all they talked about was God. I sat there, terrified, thinking this was just another waste of my time. I had heard all that "God stuff" before and figured it was never going to work for someone like me.

The Big Book talks about "contempt prior to investigation," and looking back, that's exactly what I was experiencing. I didn't even give it a chance. For months, I bounced between sober living facilities and meetings, convinced that recovery wasn't for me, all because I couldn't get past my resentments toward God. It felt like I was hitting the same wall over and over again. I didn't know it, but I would soon discover Heroin Anonymous.

On the weekend before my 26th birthday, I had dinner with my father, sister, and my daughter, who had been adopted by my sister. I was high again. It's no wonder I'd been kicked out of several sober living homes for using by then. At dinner, all I could see was an image of myself walking right back into prison and losing everything all over again, just like I had done countless times before. Every opportunity, every bit of love, every chance at a real life – I threw it all away for heroin. After dinner, I went back to the hotel where I was living and tried to get high, but the drugs didn't numb me anymore. That's when I knew I had to do something.

I hated the meetings. The idea of a God I

could trust was alien to me. But eventually, I got so miserable that I realized I had no other option. I could either try what these former drunks, junkies, and crackheads had to offer, or I could keep being miserable, just waiting to die or go back to prison.

I checked into another sober living the day before my birthday, and I didn't know what to expect. I'd been in sober living before, but this time it felt like my life depended on it. A few days in, I called a guy I'd met before and asked him if he would sponsor me. I told him I'd been getting high, and instead of being shocked, he said, "Well, it's good to hear from you. I figured you were dead." That hit me hard. I told him I was serious this time and that I was ready. I honestly didn't think it would work.

We started reading the Big Book together and working through the steps in Heroin Anonymous. I'd call him to complain about stuff, and he would basically ignore my complaints. I remember one day I got in trouble at the sober living house – I can't remember why – and I had to wash dishes for about 50 people because of it. I called my sponsor to complain, and he just said, "Maybe you'll find God in the soap. Call me back if that happens," and hung up. I'm not sure if I found God in the soap or not, but I started to realize that if the worst part of my day was washing dishes, my life was getting better.

At 60 days sober, my sponsor got me into service work. He told me to join some service committees and take on service positions. I had no clue what I was doing, but he just said, "Show up and try to be useful," so that's what I did. I started taking meetings into a detox center, joined a home group, and got introduced to the world of service. For some people, sponsorship or meetings are the core of their recovery. For me, it's always been service work.

I can't tell you how many times service work saved me. I remember sitting in a gas station parking lot with a couple of years sober, thinking about going inside to buy a beer. But I didn't because I had a service committee meeting that night. I went through a really rough patch around four years sober. I was having suicidal thoughts that no one really knew about. What kept me alive was my service work. Being accountable to the people who were relying on me gave me a reason to stay sober, a reason to keep going.

I've never taken that responsibility for granted. The people in this fellowship were there for me when I came in, and now it's my turn to be there for them. Service has always been at the heart of my recovery. It's more than just giving back – it's what keeps me connected. It reminds me that I'm not alone, that my life has meaning because of the people I get to show up for today.

When I walked into my first Heroin Anonymous meeting, a few days after getting loaded for the last time, I immediately felt at home. It was a small, dark room full of people, and I could tell that they'd lived the life I had. They weren't the "high-bottom" drunks or the "sleepless tweakers" I'd seen at other meetings. These people had been in pain, sleeping in parks, robbing their families, doing whatever it took to get well. Just like me. I was lucky enough to meet some people at that meeting who are still my best friends today, almost a decade later.

After a few years of sobriety, I found myself becoming complacent. My relationship with my sponsor had drifted – I wasn't really working with him much anymore, and I knew I needed to make a change. That's when I decided it was time to find a new sponsor, someone who could challenge me in a new way. I found a guy who had what I wanted – not in terms of money, success, or anything material like that, but in terms of spirituality, serenity, and a true sense of peace.

Over the years, he's guided me through situations I never thought I could handle sober, no matter how overwhelmed or trapped I felt in the moment. With his help, I've been able to face those challenges head-on. He's taught me how to navigate life with grace, patience, and a clear mind, something I never thought possible before. He's shown me that no matter how big the storm, I don't have to run from it or numb myself anymore. I can walk through it, one step at a time, and come out stronger on the other side.

Since getting sober, my life has changed in ways I couldn't have imagined. I have custody of my oldest daughter, who's 15 now. She's been with me since she was six because her mother struggles with addiction too. I have a great relationship with my other daughter, who I gave up for adoption – she's 13 now. And I have two beautiful sons who are four and five. I'm married to a wonderful woman who accepts me, flaws and all. I've got a career, I'm no longer a felon, and I've got a ton of friends. I even get invited to family functions again.

Heroin Anonymous saved my life in more ways than I can count. You have all given me the chance to be a father, a friend, a husband, a brother, and a son again. I've had the privilege of holding service positions and experiencing the joy that comes from being a part of this community. I'm not sure what the future holds, but I do know this: As long as I keep doing what you taught me, life will only get better.

Of course, there are still challenges. I went to jail sober because I couldn't let go of my anger. Relationships failed because of my selfishness. I lost jobs because I held on to judgment. But through helping other heroin addicts, being honest about my shortcomings, and growing my relationship with God – the same God I was so terrified of in the beginning – I've stayed sober and kept growing.

To anyone new, all I can say is this: Relax. You don't have to die to prove you don't belong. We've all been where you are, and we're here waiting for you. Maybe that sounds kind of cultish, but I'm okay with that today. When I first came into the rooms, I was absolutely terrified – of life, of sobriety, of God, of everything. I was convinced that this wouldn't work for me, that I was too far gone, too broken. I didn't think I belonged. The fear was overwhelming, and I felt like I was drowning in it. But I stayed, even when every part of me wanted to run.

I came into Heroin Anonymous thinking my

life was over, but what I found is that it was only just beginning. Today, I have real relationships, a sense of purpose and connection, and the ability to show up for my family, my friends, and myself.

This program didn't just help me get sober – it gave me a life worth living. And I'm still amazed every day that I get to be part of it. So, if you're new and terrified like I was, stick around. You don't have to have all the answers right now. Just trust that you're not alone, and give yourself the chance to experience the kind of life you never imagined possible.

One day, my sponsor asked me how I would describe God, since I was so against Him when I first came in. I thought about it for a while, and the word that came to mind was "ubiquitous." God is everywhere in my life now, and He's the reason I have everything I have today.

A SMALL TASTE OF SOBRIETY

*Heroin won every fight until this transgender
addict completed a thorough personal inventory
and made life-changing amends.*

The whole world's volume turns down, and I take a slow, shallow breath as the fuzzy warmth spreads through my chest, arms, and legs, and finally into my vacant, staring face. I lean back into the scratchy, grimy couch as the warm chemical blanket envelops every part of me. Needle still in hand and bloodstained bandanna loosely hung around my arm, I look to either side of me, where eight people are performing the same ritual. Some are quicker than others, but everyone is eager to arrive at the same destination. My eyelids drift shut and my chin sinks to my chest. I have arrived. The thought hits me, "I am a full-blown junkie now."

I had already accumulated multiple drug charges in multiple states, so you would think that this thought would have occurred to me before. Yet despite several years of daily intravenous heroin use, it hadn't. Not with the depth and weight it hit me with that day. For the past few summers, I had been shuffling around in dirty flannels to hide my track marks. Now, I didn't even try to hide them anymore. There was always at least one cigarette filter with a corner chewed off in my pack, and often a small stash of those corners, now different shades of brown and gray, stuffed behind the pack's inside wrapper. Mama always taught me to keep a reserve – you never know when a source might dry up.

I was taught how to survive by a drug addict mom and older sister in the Florida panhandle. My mom was shooting junk on the West Coast back in the 80s when she got the news that she was pregnant with me. My dad was already back in prison by the time she found out. Given this information, she decided to put down the dope, sell the bus she was living in, and move from across the country to a small Florida town on the Gulf Coast. She got involved in Alcoholics Anonymous meetings until I was seven years old. To the best of what I can recall, she relapsed around the time I was eight, but it may have been even earlier. By the time I was 13, my mom, sister, and I were getting stoned together every day. It was our family bonding time. It was just what we did and who we were. My mom and I did many drugs together over the years, and she was never able to get and stay sober for long. I keep her experience in mind when I sometimes get the idea that I can just go out for a short time and come back when I'm ready. Sounds simple, but I grew up in a house with a living example of how that story ends.

For me, it all started with a joint on a trampoline with a few other boys after a neighborhood basketball game. Over the years, I consumed any and all substances that promised any kind of relief from myself. No matter how long or brief or pleasant or distressing, I would try anything to get high. Usually more than once. From coke and benzos to huffing gas and speed pills, I didn't discriminate. I did have preferences, though, and ever since I was 15 years old, I preferred opiates. Daily use and physical dependency didn't come until my mid 20s.

Decades later, I was coming to the end of my last run. I spent every night alone in my bathroom, desperate to get high and only getting well. I just couldn't get high anymore, no matter how much I used. My last shot was in 2022, and I detoxed at home. I used a variety of drugs to ease the physical and mental discomfort. I started calling people I knew in the recovery community and got back into the rooms immediately. I sat in the back, sniffling with sunken eyes, clammy skin, and teary eyes. So many desperate prayers were made as I clenched and tried not to soil myself.

Some of the folks in those meetings already knew me, but I was more feral and withdrawn than they remembered. Desperate and broken but willing. I had come into the rooms of various 12-Step programs a handful of times over the years, always after a psych ward visit or jail sentence. My first introduction to this sober community was back in 2020. After living in my car and cheap hotels for the better part of a year, after three overdoses and a failed drug test at the probation office, I accepted an offer to stay with a friend of a friend in a famous Southern town. I had no intention of getting sober when I left Florida. I just wanted to get off the dope.

After a few days of detoxing, a thought came to me, which today, I believe was God – I had a chance to do something different this time. My intuition was telling me that if I didn't find a new path, I was going to end up in the same sorry state, only in a new place. I looked up the closest 12-Step meeting and found it was three blocks away. I was sitting in a noon meeting the next day. I only remember one thing from that first meeting – the guy who came up to me and introduced himself and told me to keep coming back. We had a short chat, and he told me he was also a heroin addict and had managed to get and stay sober through the 12 Steps. That was the first time I ever felt hope after leaving a meeting. After a few more weeks of meetings, I found my first sponsor, and we started reading the Big Book of Alcoholics Anonymous. I often needed to look up what the words meant. I found a job and a room to rent. Life was improving pretty quickly, and while I was angry and uncomfortable all the time, I didn't wanna die as often. Day by day, life didn't feel as depressing, and I was anxious less and less.

After a few months, a woman came into the meetings asking where the heroin addicts were, and a few people turned to me. She told me of a new meeting just for us junkies – a Heroin Anonymous meeting. I was skeptical at first, but I started going occasionally. It was the first meeting I ever went to where I felt I could share honestly about my experience.

In Heroin Anonymous, I kept getting to my 4th Step, and then I would relapse on weed or whiskey. One time, I got drunk and ended up smoking meth, but I was content as long as I didn't go back to shooting dope. I was in and out of the rooms until 2021. After a few months of isolation while grieving my recently deceased grandpa, I returned to my hometown for Christmas. I damn sure didn't pick up the phone to call others in the fellowship for help. I had yet to experience conscious contact with a Higher Power that wasn't a substance. So, I ended up shooting a powerful narcotic painkiller in my grandparents' house on Christmas. Guilt and shame consumed me instantly. I went on an eight-month run and picked it up like I had never stopped at all. However, that small taste of sobriety had changed me, and this time I couldn't unsee the truth of my condition. There were fleeting moments when I would try to convince myself I could manage better this time, but I knew the truth.

By 2022, I once again found myself spiritually and emotionally defeated. I was baffled at my misery because on the outside, my life was still "manageable." I had a job, a truck, and a place to live. Still, I knew the dope was going to win every time if I tried to fight it. I knew I needed help. I needed the We that I had found in the rooms, specifically Heroin Anonymous. I got a new sponsor and we got to work immediately. We read the Big Book, and I worked the 12 Steps with a willingness and open-mindedness that I had lacked before. I finally finished the 4th Step and got to share my first searching and fearless moral inventory with my sponsor. I had been completely honest and thorough. Once I got to Steps 6 and 7, I understood Step 2 more clearly. I realized that until I truly came to believe that a Higher Power could restore me to sanity, I couldn't do the work in full measure. I had known for a long time that heroin and fentanyl were a power greater than me. Through the steps, I grew to believe and trust in a Power greater than heroin. I've had spiritual experiences through the process, both large and small. Finding acceptance through faith and something more powerful than myself was what I needed.

In sobriety, I have experienced the death of my parents, job changes, the beginning and end of a loving relationship, and moved multiple times – and stayed sober through it all. By being sober, I have been able to receive treatment for my Hepatitis C and was able to begin hormone replacement therapy (HRT). I started therapy and got into a dental program to fix my teeth. I spent many months preparing to turn myself in on a probation violation warrant and possibly do jail time. I made that amends and didn't have to do jail time after all. Now, for the first time in a decade, I don't have any legal problems of any sort. Through all these moments and the many days where the old me would've turned to heroin, God and the fellowship of Heroin Anonymous were there to guide me to better decisions.

Through all these moments of progress and change, I developed an even deeper relationship with and trust in God. Daily conscious contact with the Spirit of the Universe through prayer and meditation leads me further into a truly serene life day by day. I have the ability to accept life and surrender my need to control things. I don't do it perfectly, but I sure do see progress. Getting sober and being part of this fellowship has given me the greatest gift in my life. Service to others gives me purpose, which helps me learn to love myself and others. That love and connection with others bring me closer to God. Working with other addicts and taking them through the steps has enriched my spiritual life in a way I can't describe.

I know that I only have this life today

because I'm sober. I believe the steps and the principles they teach will continue to strengthen my connection with my Higher Power. God is what keeps me sober. Every day is a choice and opportunity to stay sober and evolve my relationship with the Great Spirit. I can do that, or I can get high, and further feed my ego and devolve back into self-pity and delusion. I found God in the love and connections I've made, and it's all thanks to Heroin Anonymous.

FACING THE VOID

Leveling his pride and asking for help allowed this heroin addict to find a healing connection with a Higher Power.

Growing up, we were certainly poorer than most of the people in my town. We rarely ate out or went on trips. My mother had to make decisions like "braces OR glasses." I got glasses, and my sister got braces. My father was pretty absent in my life during my formative years, and growing up in a single-parent home definitely caused me to feel "less than." As I approached adolescence, I gravitated toward strong (and often unhealthy) male role models. I now believe that I was born with a built-in sense of separation, a core feeling that I was less than others. Sometimes, this manifests as acting or telling ourselves we are better than others, but this is just a trick we use to distract ourselves from how small we feel.

Anyways, I don't think that being lower middle class or being without a dad made me a junkie, but it did give me external evidence that confirmed the internal story I told myself – "I am less than. I am separate from."

By the time I was 13, I had developed a passion for BMX biking (one that has recently been reignited after many years off a bike), and along with this passion came long days biking around town and interacting with older kids. As I mentioned before, I was drawn to older guys who seemed confident and cool and who would give me attention. It wasn't long before my first surrogate father agreed to show me the wonders of gin and whiskey. So, I met him at a gas station in the next town over to try this magical elixir. At 13 years old and probably 100 pounds, I consumed about 12 ounces of liquor. Needless to say, I got severe alcohol poisoning and wound up in the hospital. I woke up with my mother staring at me. I got grounded for the rest of that summer. I still had wholesome friends my own age who were all very concerned. I vowed to be "straight edge" and avoid partying for life. But by the age of 15, my older BMX buddies had gotten a house in a nearby Rust Belt city, and my parents let me stay there overnight every weekend.

I almost immediately started binge drinking and began to experiment with pot. I definitely qualify as an alcoholic; I lost control every time I drank. But for me, the beginning of my rampant addiction was pot. Another one of my surrogate fathers sold high-grade marijuana and had a sweet bong. At 15, taking that first rip and feeling the immediate rush to my head, I knew I wanted to feel that way forever, and rather quickly, my life became all about chasing that euphoria. I became a daily, constant smoker, and I was acting like a junkie even with weed. Soon, I couldn't eat or sleep without it; I was using it to fight off constant headaches; I often lied, cheated, and stole to get weed. Once, I even swiped a whole bottle of painkillers to trade for a quarter-ounce.

Well, as you can imagine, this lifestyle and pursuit of euphoria led me to experiment with other drugs. One day, a friend said, "Hey, why don't you try taking one of those painkillers you're always selling us? Let me know what you think." And that is when my love affair with opioids began. That feeling of ease and comfort, that sense of being one with the world (or couch) and not caring what anyone thought – this was the best thing I had ever found to combat my internal feeling of separation. I know today that the real antidote to my problem is meaningful connection and unity with my fellows, but getting really, really high was the best I could do at the time. I dabbled with pills for the next few years, got wrapped up in the oxy epidemic, and was funneled towards snorting and then shooting heroin by my 18th birthday.

My medical paperwork says I have "polysubstance dependence," meaning I'm a total garbage head. I had periods when I was hooked on bath salts, benzos, ADHD medication, and sleeping pills. I shot coke and crack. And I always smoked weed, of course. But I know at my core I'm a junkie and a heroin addict, because that is always what I was seeking and what best filled the void.

I'll save you the full drug-o-logue, but the next three years of my life were absolute chaos. I began to lose jobs at 17 because of my use, and by 19, I was completely unemployable, with a revoked driver's license. I was in at least two drug-related car accidents before losing my license. I was involved with petty crime, hustling drugs, and then boosting, which led to a few misdemeanor arrests. I had two overdoses on heroin and benzos within a two-week period, the second of which had me in the ICU on machines for three weeks.

I went on a cross-country trip once, which ended in Ohio, when a girlfriend and I got robbed at gunpoint. I was shooting speedballs, went in and out of homelessness, and was even kicked out of one of the local shelters for being "too intoxicated."

I made some half-assed attempts at getting sober during those years. Soon after I got hooked on dope at 18, I got arrested for the first time and told my mother what I was up to. She tried really hard to get me some help. Truthfully, I was not ready to change; I just wanted a break from the chaos. I didn't want to need heroin because it was making life less fun. It was 2010, and a new type of medication-assisted treatment (MAT) was available. I remember my mother took me to a psychiatrist she thought would put me on the stuff. That doctor seemed offended and declined to prescribe me anything. I remember she told us, "With this heroin, you have crossed a bridge, you have a long road ahead of you, and you will likely relapse several times before getting sober, if you don't die first." I remember my mother crying and us storming out of there. I did my best to tell her it was nonsense and I had this under control, but man was that doctor 100% correct. When we found a doctor who would put me on MAT,

I quickly realized I could manipulate him into giving me other substances, too. My first attempt at sobriety had me on opioid replacement pills, amphetamine salts, clonazepam, and, for good measure, an antipsychotic. Heroin Anonymous has no opinion on outside issues, including MAT, and taking medicine properly prescribed by a doctor can be helpful. However, my experience was that since I wasn't ready to change, all those medications just became additional addictions, and I used them to supplement or fund my ongoing habits for marijuana and cocaine, and eventually heroin. I also had three failed attempts at outpatient treatment and two stays in inpatient rehabs.

I wish I had some cool story about a major consequence or event that led me to hit bottom, but the truth is far more gray and pathetic. By the time I was 20, my life had slowed down. I was living off of my girlfriend at the time and basically squatting in a house she "rented" in a suburb near where I grew up. Our good heroin connection had disappeared (they weren't selling heroin on every street corner back then), and so I was strung out on pills and shooting coke. Most days, I was too depressed and stuck to even commit crimes or hustle; I was tired and empty.

Once, during that period, I found myself at that same gas station where I had taken my first drink years earlier, and I saw my sister from behind. She hadn't seen me in six months and didn't know if I was alive or dead. My sister would have done anything to help me, but I couldn't face her. So, I hid from her. Not long after that, my mother snuck away to bring me food (I wasn't allowed in her home because of legitimate harm I caused my stepfather), and when I leaned over to kiss her cheek and hug her, she flinched and pulled away. I know she pulled away because of how I looked and acted, because of what I had become, but it still hurt. On one of her visits during that time, she told me, "Sometimes friends and family ask about you. How you are or where you are, and I just tell them you're lost right now."

I've told this story a hundred times, but for some reason, as I type it today, I am tearing up as I relive the pain and weight of those days, remembering the terror in my mother's face. It was these experiences and the remorse for all the damage I caused that haunted me every night. Even the drugs stopped working; sure, I could catch a buzz, but they stopped masking the void, the void that was there my whole life, making me feel separate. Not only did the drugs stop masking the void, but they had actually made it worse and led me to a situation where not only did I feel separate, but I was actually separate, alone, and hopeless.

Within a few weeks, I had a moment of clarity. After a routine dispute with my girlfriend, I started to experience strange thoughts. Thoughts like, "Hey, you should just leave and try to get some help." I know today that this was my Higher Power – my conscience, my higher self, whatever you want to call it. I had once been a good kid. I had a baseline of kindness and honesty, and I knew right from wrong, but this conscience was always blotted out by my ego and my false sense of being worse than or better than, which required an insatiable amount of drugs to keep quiet. But for whatever reason, I was blessed to hear those thoughts on that day, to have that moment of clarity and actually act on it. I don't know why some of us get these chances to make a change and so many of us die without this opportunity, but I thank God every day that He was there when I was ready, and I do my best not to spoil this gift.

I remembered my sister's phone number and called her for help that day. She showed up and helped me buy supplies to move in with some friends. She even helped cover up my track marks with makeup, so I wouldn't look as rough to those friends. That was all on April 20, 2012, which would have been a cool sobriety date, but I was still delusional. I thought sobriety was just about changing my environment and avoiding hard drugs. So, I made a ton of changes, and I figured my marijuana and benzos maintenance plan would keep me on the straight and narrow. You'll be shocked to learn that this approach did not work for me, and I came out of a blackout about a month later in yet another homeless shelter, where they were explaining that I was being kicked out for violating their rules and testing positive for hard drugs.

This was in 2012, and it was the day I finally surrendered. It finally hit me that deciding to change wasn't enough. For the first time ever, I wanted to be sober, and I was afraid because I didn't know how. The shelter workers took pity on me and allowed me to stay for another 40 days while I got into a halfway house. For the first few weeks, I was placed on lockdown and only allowed to leave to attend a 12-Step meeting up the street. This is where my journey began.

I always thought religion and spirituality were for dumb people who were afraid of what would happen when they die. I had been introduced to 12-Step programs in rehab but avoided them because of the spiritual component. But something changed for me when I hit bottom; I didn't have any arguments left. I started to see that the people in meetings were sober and happy at the same time, and they all prayed and talked about God. People complain about early sobriety, but it was one of the best summers of my life. I didn't have to work; I got into a halfway house and fell in with a good group of guys. Because I was the youngest and smallest, I fell into the familiar role of seeking surrogate fathers, and though they hazed me a bit, they really looked out for me. The guys in that house were making it their business to stay sober, and a core group of us would go to two meetings every day.

I found meetings frequented by younger folks who were accepting of drug talk, and I found a home. I looked for other junkies who looked and acted like me at meetings, and I stuck with them. While being physically sober and going to meetings made my life better, that internal feeling of being less than was still alive and well. I had several close calls with relapse in my first four months and obsessed about using every day. I remember scheming ways to try and steal my roommate's meds to get high and staring at my healthy veins in meetings, fantasizing about hitting them. I was so full of fear, and my ego, that false sense of self, kept me from letting the fellowship love me or help me fully. One of the few people I let get close to me saw that I was fading away, and he bullied me into getting a sponsor. He said, "You're going to all these 12-

Step meetings, and you aren't even working the 12 Steps. You're going to die."

So, at four months sober, I asked a guy to sponsor me, and that's when things really began to change. I began to take two buses across town so that my sponsor could read the Big Book with me. He would stop at specific points, elaborate, ask questions, and then, sometimes, he would give me assignments. Looking back, the first gift the steps gave me was that sometime around taking my 3rd Step, the obsession to use was removed from me. Sure, I have triggers – I am a junkie, and sometimes things remind me of drugs – but the craving, that overwhelming desire to get high, has been removed for the last 12 years. I didn't understand it at the time, but leveling my pride and asking for help, having the humility to take direction, opening up to a Higher Power, and letting my sponsor and fellows show me love were beginning to heal my void.

The inventory steps helped me get down to causes and conditions, and to uncover the faulty ways of thinking and acting, the out-of-whack fears and relationships that were driving me. The amends process allowed me to face the demons that kept me up at night and slay them with the proper tools. I have also experienced someone refusing my amends. My stepfather, to this day, will not accept my amends. We don't speak, and I'm not allowed over to my mom's house when he is home. But that's okay. I cleaned my side of the street, and I am free from the shame of what I did. The amends process also helped me to heal my relationship with my biological father, and he is one of my best friends today.

I really think the steps work by taking the most selfish and delusional people on earth, junkies like you and me, and cleaning us up enough to be capable of loving and serving others. And as soon as we are ready, we live in Step 12, where we have a life dependent on service to others. When I live a life that is full of service to others, I don't fall back into my void of separation. Step 12 has been a huge part of my life since I was about nine months sober and began looking for sponsees. On average, I have five to 10 people I sponsor at any given time.

I had a large home group with a ton of people my age, and they all had what I wanted – cars, apartments, relationships, and, most importantly, they radiated joy and peace. I desperately wanted what these people had, so I had to do what they did. I was just over 21 years old, and I didn't know anything about life. I learned how to tie a tie because I had to speak at our speaker meeting; I learned to send an email because I needed to make a report for a service committee; I got a job because I wanted to stop mooching off my friends when we went to fellowship at the diner after our meetings. That community gave me a design for living that truly set me up for success. Before I was two years sober, I was studying the concepts and traditions. I had become employable, gotten my license back, and even had my first sober girlfriend.

For me, life was good, but it was 2017, and now the opioid epidemic was in full swing. I was five years sober, and because of my foundation in that home group, I was deeply entrenched in district and area service for a 12-Step fellowship. We were seeing dear friends dying left and right from heroin and fentanyl, and then we heard about this new meeting called Heroin Anonymous, which had started in a neighboring city. We were skeptical at first, but one night, I attended this H.A. meeting with a few of my home group members. I instantly fell in love with Heroin Anonymous. I saw a program that used the approach I trusted (the Twelve Steps) but gave a safe place for us to speak junkie.

Within a month, we started the first H.A. meeting in our city. The original meeting had over 60 people, standing room only, every Tuesday for an entire year until the fellowship spread out and more meetings started up. We had a strong group conscience and tried to set an example for service, which carried to the H.A. groups that followed. Members from that first meeting also formed the service body that eventually became An Area Group of Heroin Anonymous. Some of those same members later helped host the H.A. World Convention, and it was a great success.

Everything I have in this world, every skill I've learned, came from doing service. I only know how to love because I was taught how to serve. If you feel you aren't getting enough from your meetings, if you feel separate, then look for a committee or a group that needs help, become a group service representative, or join a conference committee and give it your all. I promise you will not be disappointed. I am eternally grateful to all of you, for it is through service and staying connected to my fellows that I can finally feel whole. All I need to do today is look around at my friends in the program and do my service work, and I know without a doubt that I am no longer separate. I have a home in Heroin Anonymous.

I can promise you this: if you want what we have and do what we do, you can live a life of love and service, and you don't ever have to use again.

LOST AT SEA

*He was chewed up and spit out by addiction,
but he was alive – and that was all he
needed to make a beginning in H.A.*

It was the beginning of 2021, during the height of COVID, when it happened. I had found myself on a boat out to sea somewhere off the coast of Southern California. It was early, and the sun wasn't even up yet. We were coming out of a thunderous rainstorm that rocked the boat all hours of the night as we sat anchored in the water. Rain, leaking through the ceiling and dropping on my face, kept waking me up. It was like Chinese water torture. I was in a pretzel position, cold, miserable, and curled up sideways in the galley trying to sleep, but I couldn't. To add insult to injury, I had a clear view into the captain's bedroom, where I could see my ex-fiancé asleep with her new boyfriend. It was a constant reminder of the life I no longer shared with the woman I once loved. Just a year ago, we had been set to marry, and now here we were. Addiction had torn us apart.

I suppose my addiction really started at 14 years of age, when my parents divorced. My father had left, and I chose to stay with my mother. Soon afterward, I started drinking whenever alcohol was present. Meanwhile, my mother found herself newly engaged to an established doctor with his own family practice. It was during that time that I discovered pain pills. My mother would bring them home from the practice she managed for him, along with a goodie bag of other narcotics from pharmaceutical reps. She would leave them around the house for me to find, and I tried them all. In those years, alcohol and pills kept me going. They went together like peas and carrots. All the while, I was suppressing problems I didn't know how to manage. This became my go-to remedy for a long time.

At 18 years old, I moved out, ready to take on the world. I had become a master functioning addict, and I thought I could deal with almost anything. Eventually, I landed a successful gig in the music scene, where I discovered cocaine. After that little discovery, I had officially found my *recipe*. The perfect combination of pain pills and cocaine. Anytime these two drugs danced together, they brought out my inner superhero, the best version of myself, or so I thought.

For a time, life seemed good for a functioning addict like me. And toward the end of my music career, as we finished our last tour, I met my soon-to-be fiancé. We had both played in established bands for several years before we met, and we felt an immediate connection with one another. Simply put, we fell in love. Although it was difficult to part ways from our bands, together we were beginning a new chapter in our lives. It was time to move on, and we were ready to settle down and start a life together. And for 10 long years, we did just that! We had the house, the cars, a couple little dogs running around, and a successful business we built together to pay the bills. We were happy, stable, and somehow managed our addiction through it all. I was confident I had a controlled grip on everything, and so I decided to propose to her. Although she said yes, my confidence was soon shaken as my addiction took a turn for the worse, and quickly.

Shortly after the proposal, my life would unravel. I would lose my mother to cancer, dive deeper into my addiction, lose my house, my possessions, my cars, my friends, my business, and all my employees. Eventually, I isolated myself from my family while I drifted further into my disease.

By this point I no longer had the luxury of buying pills and cocaine. I immediately jumped ship and switched over to heroin and speed, using both regularly and aggressively. Soon, I lost my fiancé to another guy, one final gut punch on the way down the ladder of doom. The hits just kept coming. Eventually, I found myself at the bottom. I wound up homeless on the streets, stealing from department stores and committing petty theft just to survive, all while getting into fentanyl.

I was broken and alone in the absolute abyss of addiction. For three years, I lived in a perpetual state of misery, handcuffed to this disease, living to die, dying to live. I needed a way out and needed help fast. Not long after, I ran into my ex again, now with her new boyfriend, who captained a sailboat nearby. Reluctantly, I accepted their invitation to stay on the boat for a few nights to rest my head. Instead, we partied the night away, just the three of us, consuming every drug known to man. All of us in denial, pretending this wasn't awkward, while a storm was brewing on the horizon, heading straight for us.

So, there I lay, wide awake, helpless, and

heartbroken. The boat was rocking so hard in the storm I was sure it would soon sink, yet I was paralyzed with the crushing feeling of defeat. I was cold and confused, stuck on a soon-to-be sunken boat, which reflected the miserable reality I now lived in. How did I get here? And if the boat did represent some kind of metaphor, at what point did I stop sailing, throw the anchor overboard, and just give up?

My restless mind continued to grapple with these questions. I began to reflect, putting every decision I ever made (for better or for worse) on trial, desperately trying to arrive at some kind of verdict to make sense of everything.

And then ... the rain stopped. The storm subsided, and the sun rose on calm waters. All the noise in my head, all the reminders of my failures, just turned off, and suddenly ... there was *peace*. In that moment, I felt the *hand of God* lift the veil of my reality as the world came to a stop. I was given a glimpse of the life that waited for me on the other side of all my pain. What I saw that morning would soon change everything. I saw a man with a paintbrush standing in front of a blank canvas that represented a world of endless opportunities. He was just standing there, brush in hand, ready to paint. He looked eager and anxious, like he'd been standing there for a long time. He showed me his vision of a life waiting to be lived. A life filled with light and love without limits that existed outside the realm of darkness. A life of principle.

For the first time, I felt hope. I could see a life worth living, finally within my reach. There was no more doubt or fear. It was as if God himself wrapped a warm blanket of reassurance around me with absolute clarity and certainty. That warmth felt more real and powerful than *any* other high I had spent my life chasing. The vision I saw that morning was so clear that it gave me the willingness I needed to take one of the biggest leaps of faith I would ever take.

After that profound moment of clarity, I took a few minutes to come back and gather myself. It was about that time that everyone on the boat was waking up and moving around to start the day. When the captain of the boat was in the galley making breakfast, I got up and quickly pulled him aside. I immediately thanked him for his hospitality in posting me up for a few nights. Furthermore, I acknowledged how awkward it was for the three of us to be under the same roof for too long. I chose to share with him my recent revelation and asked him for an unconventional favor – I needed to get sober quickly and then part ways. He could have said no, but he agreed to my plan and allowed me to stay on his boat for a few more nights to white-knuckle my way through a painful detox from multiple drugs. He promised to keep me anchored out to sea away from shore and out of harm's way. Basically, I temporarily handcuffed myself in isolation to prevent any moments of weakness while I was kicking. It felt like I spent weeks on that boat. Minutes felt like hours, and hours felt like days. I was delirious in every sense of the word. I would spend the most challenging few days and nights of my life on that boat, fighting heroin, speed, fentanyl, alcohol, coke, weed, pills, and even cigarettes, all at once!

I would be lying if I said I felt 100% better by the end of the week. In fact, I felt far from it. But I was clean, and no longer kicking. It was now time for me to leave the boat and head for shore.

Although still a bit foggy and restless, I remember feeling a determination and confidence I had never felt before. It was a very strange feeling. In some ways, it was similar to my first experiences with alcohol and drugs, yet this was something much different, something more raw and potent than any drug I had ever consumed.

Now, don't get me wrong. I was still a broken man. I was vulnerable, weighed down by insecurities and problems I knew I would have to face at some point. But I was clean! I was ready to take on the world again in a whole new light. And with that, I stepped ashore. My feet left the boat and hit the sand, and I felt peace. There was a new horizon of possibilities in sight, even though I knew the journey ahead of me could be just as challenging as the one behind me.

I immediately found a phone and called my brother, a recovering addict with 20 years in sobriety. He got a one-way ticket for me on the earliest train out of town. He lived an hour away, and I couldn't have run fast enough to make sure I got to the train before it left the station. I hadn't seen my brother in years since I fell off the grid. Sure enough, my brother was there to pick me up. His family took me in for a few nights to help me get on my feet. It was very emotional to see my family again. I went to church the following day with the whole family. I was introduced to a handful of people and immediately felt at home. To my surprise, I quickly learned that 90% percent of the congregation were people in recovery who suffered from the same disease of addiction that I had. Even the pastor himself, sporting scars and tattoos up and down his body, shared a story I quickly identified with. He spoke with such truth and conviction while he passionately delivered his message to the church. I decided to plant my feet solidly in God's will rather than my own and prayed for guidance. Soon after, a friend of my brother took me to my first H.A. meeting.

It was not easy to walk into my first meeting, but I kept thinking about something I heard in church that day. "Faith without works is dead." I had to resist the urge to walk away from the meeting. For many years, whenever I felt uncomfortable in a situation, I would immediately leave unannounced. I had become a very good escape artist.

The few times I tried to leave the meeting, my surroundings seemed to shift. When I did try to walk away, I was approached by a couple, and I felt an immediate connection with them. I felt a sense of compassion, empathy, and care. I felt understood, and most of all, I felt acceptance with a sense of belonging. I sat with them and my new friend who brought me in. I was told to listen and observe, and I did just that. The longer I sat and listened, the more comfortable I began to feel. I'd soon understand that I wasn't alone, and I had finally found my tribe.

As I slowly regained my faith in God and His will, I began to notice Him working in my life. I was advised by my brother to immediately get a sponsor and do 90 meetings in 90 days. I didn't know how that would be possible with no dependable transportation. My brother scoffed and said, "All you have to do is ask, and watch the miracle unfold." I soon realized how easy it was. Sure enough, every single day, and sometimes even two or three times a day, I would somehow, by the grace of God, get to a meeting and back home again. Most of the time, I got rides from people I barely knew, and sometimes I'd never see them again after they dropped me off. I was in total awe of the hospitality I felt from people in recovery. It was so refreshing to experience that level of unconditional love.

I realized that we don't have to do this alone. We have all the support we will ever need through the guidance of our Higher Power.

For me, doing the 90 in 90 was essential to build the solid foundation I needed for my recovery. I decided that no matter how reclusive or awkward I felt at times, I would always introduce myself to two or more people at every single meeting and get their phone numbers. By doing that, I quickly created my recovery family, gained new friends, and built relationships. With those relationships, I could finally trade my insecurities for confidence in who I am.

As I share this glimpse into my story, I want to encourage the newcomer who might be reading this. It was four years ago that I found recovery through Heroin Anonymous. I walked through the doors to my first H.A. meeting with nothing but the clothes on my back. I was homeless, hopeless, and bankrupt spiritually, mentally, and emotionally. I had been chewed up and spit out, but I was alive, and that's all I needed to make a beginning in Heroin Anonymous.

Four years later, I genuinely believe I am building and living the life I was meant to live. I am closer to my family than I have ever been. My bills are paid, my credit is good (both on paper and in real life), I have my own place, a brand-new car, and a secure job. I'm in the best health of my life, eating right, working out, and seeing a special someone in recovery who shares my vision for life. Most importantly, I'm clean, with both feet planted firmly in God's will, living my purpose one day at a time with the strongest support system I have ever known.

My advice to all my recovering friends: Let the path behind you be all the strength you need for the one in front of you. Let go and let God, have faith, trust in the process, and most importantly, never give up! Everything you've ever wanted is just on the other side of the door, along with a family waiting to support you. The door has been left unlocked, just waiting to be opened.

Blessings.

INDIGENOUS, SOBER, AND FREE

Raised on an Indian reservation, she walked through a hell of abuse and trauma to overcome her addiction.

I was born in upstate New York in 2002 and raised on a nearby Indian reservation. Growing up on the reservation, drinking and drug use were common. My mother knew this. She had her own problems with substances but managed to remain abstinent for her children. My mother was strict, but she had good reasons. I see now that my mother was doing her best to protect her children from substance abuse. Although she was trying to protect us, she also scared us through verbal, physical, and mental abuse. As a child I was confused. The person I loved and trusted was hurting me.

The first time I drank alcohol, I was 13. That first drink was euphoric, and I was willing to do whatever I could to escape my mother's abuse. The more I drank, the more defiant I became. When my mother finally had enough, she let me move into my father's home. After my father gained custody of me, I took advantage of his kindness and love. I started using more than ever before, any chance I could. My whole high school experience, I used any and everything I could get my hands on – alcohol, pills, acid, cocaine, molly. But never heroin or crack. I would never be a low-life junkie.

In my junior year of high school, I found myself in a relationship with someone older than me, who was more experienced in drug use and drinking. We bonded over drinking and smoking weed. I can see now that this man was preying on me. He knew I was coming into some money when I turned 18, and a month after my 18th birthday, he started using heroin more frequently around me. Naturally, I became curious about the drug he was using. I saw his obsession and sense of relief when putting the lighter to the foil. I asked to try the drug, and he said no. I replied, "Then this is the last time I'm buying it for you." He said nothing at first, then handed me the foil.

The feeling of smoking heroin was like nothing I'd ever felt before. I was always irritable, discontent, and anxious, but when heroin hit my system, I was instantly hooked. I had finally found what I was looking for. I had arrived.

After using for weeks on end, the relationship became very toxic, and we started to fight more. Every day he beat me black and blue, but I chose to stay for heroin. I was willing to stay in a relationship that was life-threatening because my boyfriend was my only connection. The minute I found my own connection, I left my boyfriend, jumping right out a second-floor window and running straight to the trap house. My cousin was there, and he vouched for me, so they let me move in. The next day my ex showed up, kicking in the door. I woke up to my cousin and ex-boyfriend fist fighting. I locked the door and hid in the back room until the fight was over. I know the only reason he showed up was because I stole his phone and whatever money he had left, but it was already gone by the time he got there.

I continued to steal from everyone around me, selling fake bags and burning bridges whenever I could. Soon enough, I wasn't welcome anywhere. I moved off the reservation to a nearby town, where I found new connections. I went all over the city, ripping and running, going in and out of toxic relationships, staying only when they had something to offer me. Nothing was genuine. The more people I met, the more I learned about hustling the streets. By 19 I was running pockets, driving drug dealers between states, car hopping, scrapping metal and copper, and selling my body for heroin. I was willing to do anything to get heroin.

At this point, I was on autopilot; the car was driving, but nobody was in the driver's seat. A couple of months after I turned 20, I was introduced to the needle. Before using the needle, I always told myself, "That will never be me." Well, all it took was one bad night for me to become exactly that.

One night, I showed up to the trap house, and a man who had preyed on me before was there with his girlfriend. I went to the bathroom to try to scrape my straw and bubble, but there was barely anything left. I was still dopesick. When I came out of the bathroom, I caught his girlfriend stealing my corner store hat. I confronted her and figured she would give it back. It was just a cheap $10 hat. She gave the hat back, but the second I turned around, she punched me in the back of my head, and we started to fight. I kicked her and she flew back, landing on top of a half-broken tweaker table. She pulled a knife and started threatening me, but I didn't even care if she stabbed me. If I got stabbed, either I would finally die, or I'd be injured badly enough that the hospital would have to prescribe me pain meds. Finally, her boyfriend threw her out of the house. Now he had me alone. Not only was I dopesick, but now I was filled with adrenaline and all kinds of emotions I didn't want to feel. I was dry heaving in the bathroom when he pulled a needle out. He told me my pain would be relieved by one hit. I asked if he had anything I could smoke, but he said it was the needle or nothing. I was sick and ready to get my fix, so I agreed.

I handed him my arm.

I was so scared and in so much pain that I was willing to trust a predator to shoot me up with drugs. When the shot went through my veins, I felt a warmth spread through my feet, ears, hands, and throat. My mouth watered. Whatever sense of self I still had was now gone, and nothing else mattered. I couldn't move. I remember he laid me down and removed my pants and panties. He used me for hours. When he finally left and I could move again, I pretended nothing had happened. My only concern was finding my next high. I had become an IV heroin user.

I continued using the needle, sleeping on

couches covered with roaches and bed bugs, breaking into abandoned homes, and wearing the same clothes for days at a time. The way I was living, I couldn't sleep. If I did, men would try to touch me in my sleep, or other addicts would rummage through my bags. I had to stay awake, no matter what. I slowly started falling into psychosis. My life had become unmanageable a long time ago, but now I was racing toward a true bottom. I was full of envy, hate, jealousy, self-pity, and negative thoughts. The rotten person I had become on the inside was now manifesting on the outside. I had scab picks all over my body and my clothes were dirty from top to bottom. I smelled horrible. I was bone skinny. But still heroin was calling my name. The more I used, the stronger and more animated my psychosis became. I saw things you could only see in a horror movie. Voices started giving me commands, the most important of which was to kill myself. I tried to do exactly that several times, but before each attempt, I had to get high one more time. Who knows how many times I told myself, "If I'm going to die, I'm going to be high." I was the walking dead, living under a bridge or sleeping on park benches, dragging this shell of a body to get one more fix. I had become a low-life junkie.

As long as I got high, it was a good day. The thought of getting sober never crossed my mind. One day, I robbed a drug dealer of a good amount of heroin and meth, put it on foil, and smoked it. The rest went in my bra. I had my father pick me up shortly after that. He took me to a large tribal ceremony with over 70 people, and I spent most of my time in the portable toilet getting high. My dad and his friends all knew I was high, and they followed me everywhere I went. I was very annoyed. I did not want their help. I just needed to get out of town for a bit. Well, at least until my supply was gone, then I'd go back to the city.

At one point, my dad called me into the arbor (the center of the ceremony). He took me to the tree that everyone had been praying around. He had me put my head on the tree and told me to pray. For one second, I felt a power greater than myself, and I prayed. I asked for help, and I genuinely cried for the first time I could remember. I knew I needed help. I was only 20 years old, which meant my father had legal say over my life until I turned 21. He had me involuntarily admitted into the psych ward. I was pissed, but there was nothing I could do about it. I was able to sneak my drugs into the facility, but they only lasted me the first night. By the second day, I started to detox. I'd been dopesick before, but the fact that I couldn't do anything about it drove me even more insane.

When I got out of the psych ward, I was still sick and determined to get back to the city. I manipulated my dad into taking me back, and I copped more drugs. My father tried several more institutions and psych wards, but I would always manipulate my way out of them. Finally, he found an out-of-state rehab with an open bed, and he drove me there. I stayed for a couple weeks until my monthly allowance hit my account, and the day it did, I left. Back home, I picked up right where I left off, digging deeper and deeper. One day, I called my dad to come get me, and he said no. I could hear the pain in his voice, and it hurt me too. Finally, all my connections, bridges, and relationships had been burned due to my addiction. I had run out of options. The only option I had was to get sober.

I admitted myself into a rehab and tried to hold onto life. Out of all the groups and meetings they made us go to, only one caught my attention. They called it a 12-Step meeting. It wasn't the steps that caught my attention at first, but the fact that someone well-dressed, well-spoken, and confident shared their story, and it was similar to mine. At first, I convinced myself that the person sharing was full of lies. There was no way this person who used like me would come here and do this for free simply out of the goodness of their heart. Even though I thought it might be a bunch of BS, I also thought maybe there was a way out of this hell after all. So, I took the suggestions and continued my journey.

I moved to a 90-day rehab and a woman came in. She said she was doing service for H.A., and she shared her story – my story. I was very interested in what she had to say, so I took more suggestions and moved into a halfway house. To live there, I had to attend 12-Step meetings and get a sponsor. I did exactly that, and suddenly I wasn't alone anymore. There really was a way out.

I was willing to do whatever it took to live in recovery. Something greater than me was doing something I couldn't do for myself. Day by day, I learned to sit with myself and how to cope using healthy methods. I was on a roll. I went home for my 21st birthday to visit my mom, and she was very sick. It had been six years since she saw me sober, and I got the privilege to look her in her eyes with an open heart and a clear mind and tell her I love her. A month later, she passed away. For a while after her funeral, I woke up every day thinking about the needle. "Faith without works is dead," I told myself. So, every time I wanted to use, I talked to someone and went to meetings to hear the message. I finally started working the steps with my sponsor. I knew shooting dope wasn't going to bring Mom back, and so I stayed resilient and held on. Continuously working the program and leaning on the fellowship has worked wonders in my life, and it will work wonders in yours.

I'm not ashamed of what I went through. Today, thanks to the program of H.A., I have the life I prayed for before my addiction started. I had to walk through hell to get to my heaven. Today, I am of service to H.A. Today, I recover loudly for those who use heroin in silence. Today, I am free from heroin.

FINDING SERENITY
WHERE I LEAST
EXPECTED

When the pain of existing became too much, this heroin addict had to embrace a spiritual solution in order to survive.

I grew up in a suburban household in the Northeast with an alcoholic father and a mother with severe mental health problems. I don't remember much of anything from my early childhood. There was a lot of fighting, so I guess dissociating was my way of coping with all of that. From what I was told, Dad threatened to burn the house down with all of us in it, so Mom left on his birthday while he was at work. She took me and my sister to live with my grandparents. My mother was suicidal at this point. She was getting electric shock therapy treatments to help with the severity of her depression, leaving her bedridden. I have a very distinct memory of trying to go into her room to see her and my grandmother stopping me and saying, "Mommy's sleeping." As a 5-year-old kid, I thought this was all my fault.

"There's something wrong with me," "I don't deserve love," and "I don't belong here" were all common thoughts. Dad was limited to Sunday visitations, which was later turned into supervised visitations, which then turned into no visitations. The story behind that is he took my sister and me to his local watering hole and left us in the car while he went in for a drink.

We did a decent amount of moving around until Mom was able to get on her feet as a single mother. Wherever we went, I felt so uncomfortable in my own skin. Riddled with anxiety and depression, I just wanted to feel any form of ease or comfort. When I was in seventh grade, a cool older boy asked me to ditch class with him. This was the fork-in-the-road moment for me. Older kids were allowed to go out into town for lunch, but I was just a seventh-grader heading to math class. If you haven't already guessed, I went with him. I was with the cool kids now. I had arrived! Shortly after that day, I was offered my first mind-altering substance – pot. I finally felt that ease and comfort that I was looking for. From that point on, I was off to the races.

All I wanted to do at that point in my life was skateboard, smoke pot, dabble with other party drugs, and ditch school as much as possible. By the time I was 15, I was arrested and sent to a mental hospital to be evaluated. It was deemed appropriate by the courts to send me to a therapeutic boarding school. I spent months in different juvenile facilities until a bed opened up for me. Once I got to the therapeutic boarding school, I was surrounded by other troubled teenagers. I decided to focus my studies there on drugs and how many of them I could take. I eventually got kicked out of the boarding school after getting sent to multiple mental institutions to be re-evaluated. Back home and waiting for a bed to open up in an even stricter facility, I found opiates for the first time. All the other drugs I tried were great, but this... this was it! It was the warm hug I never got from Mom when I was just a scared 5-year-old kid.

When I got to my new boarding school, I became incredibly sick. It was like the worst flu I ever had, times a million. All I remember was taking as many baths as I could in an absolutely disgusting bathtub, with no care that it looked like it hadn't been cleaned for 100 years. I had no clue at this point, but this was my first experience with kicking opiates.

Soon after, I turned 18 and was able to sign myself out. I took all my belongings in a huge garbage bag and hopped on the first bus to Grand Central Station. I then had to "carry" that bag from Grand Central to Penn Station. I was still weak from kicking, so I dragged the bag more than I carried it. Right in the middle of Penn Station, with thousands of people buzzing past, the bag ripped, and my stuff scattered all over the floor. Luckily, a janitor walked past and gave me another garbage bag. I finally made it to a friend's house, which was more like a trap house. I had my very own mattress on the floor, though. I was finally free! There were no rules at this house. The name of the game was to do as many drugs as we could find, opioids being number one. This was during the oxy era, and when the pills became too expensive, my friends introduced me to heroin. At this point, heroin was the closest I had ever felt to God. At this time in my life, if you asked me what my thoughts were on a Higher Power, I would have told you, "I hate God! I didn't do anything to deserve a childhood like this."

My bright idea at this point was to move back to my mother's house, get on opioid medication maintenance, and continue with my other drug use. At least with this medication, I was basically getting free heroin from the government, I thought. I nurtured a pretty gnarly cocaine habit and was six-foot-four and about 125 pounds. There were many moments when I felt like I was dying. I saw the light fading in my eyes. This was the first time I had ever acknowledged that I had a real problem.

I had an uncle in California with a history of substance use. I decided I would make a geographical change and live with him. I brought the last of my cocaine with me through the airport and onto the plane. In the insanity of my disease, this seemed totally rational. I finished my coke in the airplane bathroom, and I made it to California without getting arrested. I managed to get off all the drugs, but I was still taking my medically assisted treatment. Even though I was now on the other side of the country, I had brought myself with me, and I felt more alone than ever before. I managed to run into some of my old friends who had also moved to the West Coast, and I latched onto them for dear life. Maybe too much so. They were all successful adults with careers, and I was working for my uncle, doing whatever odd jobs he was kind enough to find for me. I couldn't help but compare myself to them, and once again, I felt less-than. Still, I was doing my best to make it work.

Then came my 21st birthday. I had only drunk a handful of times before this. The first time, I was about 13 years old, and I drank a beer and a half and threw up. I stuck with the drugs from that point on, but now the drugs weren't a viable option. My friends assured me that they would make me drinks that tasted good. The drinks were more than good. Turns out, I had never figured out that I was a liquor guy and not a beer guy. I drank all night with guys who had been drinking heavily for many years. I saw nothing wrong with it because, hey... I wasn't doing heroin or smoking crack. It's just alcohol.

I ended up moving back home. I started working better jobs, I got an actual high school diploma, got my driver's license, and got off the medication-assisted treatment. It was the worst kick of my life times a million. It took me a month before I felt better physically, and six months before I felt better mentally. (I didn't go off my medication under a doctor's direction; I did it "my way," as always.)

I was no longer a slave to my opioid addiction (or so I thought). Right around this time, my drinking started to get worse. I became very close with my father, as we finally had something in common. We became drinking buddies, and he showed me how to drink like a true alcoholic. Whiskey for breakfast. Alcoholism later took my father's life, as it did his father's, and his father's before him. When he was dying, I had the power of attorney for him, and so I had to "pull the plug," as suggested by his doctors. My alcoholism continued to worsen and spiral. I got a DUI after I blacked out behind the wheel and woke up in the back of a police car. By the time I got to the hospital, my BAC was 0.42. I fought the case for about a year, then decided it was time to return to California – not to stop drinking, of course, but to get a job doing some "manly" work. Without a college education, I figured this was my only option.

I ended up scuba diving, scraping barnacles off boat bottoms. I was making good money, had an apartment, and even girlfriends. I told myself I was doing okay. This narrative boosted my ego and made me believe it was acceptable to drink from morning until night and even start doing cocaine again. But then something changed. The ease and comfort I had once received from drinking started to disappear. Drinking began to worsen my anxiety and depression – the very reason I started using substances in the first place. I became unable to leave my bedroom. The thought of going to the bathroom in the next room, in the safety of my own apartment, filled me with anxiety.

After a few days, I decided to take my own life. The pain of existing was so unbearable that stabbing myself four times and enduring 34 staples and 32 stitches seemed less painful. I bled out in my bathtub for hours, but God had different plans for me. My neighbor and friend, who understood addiction and mental health, came to my rescue and saved my life.

I found myself back in the psych ward, where they offered me opioids for the pain of my wounds. Even though I had been opioid free for seven years and had promised myself I would never do opioids again, I decided not to disclose my prior addiction. After all, I never tried to kill myself because of my opioid addiction, I told myself. This soon spiraled into a whirlwind of drug smuggling, crack smoking, fentanyl overdoses, and even falling asleep underwater while scuba diving to clean a boat. I somehow managed not to get arrested or killed, and God soon put a wonderful woman into my life. I put her through absolute hell, but somehow she stuck around.

We spent eight months living in a van and traveling the country, visiting different national parks. I wasn't using and was surrounded by the most beautiful sights Mother Earth could offer, but at night, all I could think about was getting loaded. Our trip ended at a friend's place in the mountains. That night, my friend offered me cocaine, not knowing I was "sober" and white-knuckling. With my girlfriend around, I kindly said, "No, thank you." But the next morning, while my girlfriend was asleep in the van with her cat, I rummaged through my friend's room until I found his stash and freebased most of it in his bathroom.

Soon, I was freebasing cocaine, smoking crack, and using opioids again. When I had to attend my grandma's funeral, I had to swallow a fistful of benzos just to level myself out. At this time, my girlfriend and I were still traveling constantly, but wherever we went, my addiction and obsession to use followed me. When I couldn't get hard drugs, I started buying kratom and taking it daily, becoming a slave to yet another mind-altering substance. Eventually, my girlfriend had enough of my addiction, and I was alone again. I was also free to use drugs however I liked. I sold my possessions and spent it all on fentanyl and crack. But just like with alcohol, eventually, even these powerful drugs stopped working. I was left with nothing but the urge to die. This was in 2022. I cried out to the universe for help. God answered my prayer, but not in the way I expected. Instead of taking away my addiction, God granted me the "gift of desperation." I finally accepted, with every ounce of my being, that I was powerless over drugs and alcohol and that my life had become unmanageable – my first First Step experience.

I admitted myself to a crisis house. I once again found myself crying hysterically on a filthy bathroom floor, sick from withdrawal. I realized that no matter what mind-altering substance I took, I always ended up in the same place, living out the same vicious cycle of hurting those who loved me, losing everything, and wanting to die alone.

Eventually, I entered a treatment center, broken enough to be willing to do whatever it took. I was no longer trying to get clean "my way." I found myself surrounded by men who had been through what I had, some worse, some not as bad, but we all shared the same spiritual malady. These men loved me until I could love myself. God was working through them, giving me "good orderly direction." They taught me honesty, open-mindedness, and willingness. They introduced me to the Big Book and other recovery literature, showed me the steps, and taught me the importance of getting a sponsor and finding a fellowship. They were a "group of drunks," or "group of degenerates," helping me find a God of my own understanding.

From these men, I learned kindness, acceptance, and all the spiritual principles of the fellowship. It was up to me to put these teachings into action. I went "meeting shopping" to expand my community and attended various meetings. One day, I asked a friend if she knew of any good meetings, and she recommended Heroin Anonymous. From my first visit, I felt at home. These people were just like me. They were working to grow spiritually. I soon found a sponsor and an even bigger family.

In Heroin Anonymous, I fully accepted my powerlessness over drugs and alcohol. I found a Higher Power that I now realize has always been with me, an infinite energy source that exists in everything. I learned to trust in God, recognizing that I can only control my actions and reactions – sometimes not even that. I learned that outside issues don't have to be my business if I don't want them to be. I took a detailed look at my life, facing my mistakes and the harm I had caused myself and others. I let go of the lies I had been telling myself and embraced the good in me while striving to cast the bad parts aside.

I developed humility, asking God to help me with these negative thoughts and learn new ways of thinking. I learned the value of hard work and patience in achieving lasting success in life. I examined the people I had harmed and understood that saying "sorry" wasn't enough. To truly make amends, I couldn't repeat my past mistakes. I learned to be mindful of my actions and not to rely so heavily on my mind, where my disease lives. Instead, I learned to listen to my heart.

Practicing meditation, I developed a 90-second rule: If I find myself stuck on a thought for more than 90 seconds, I call my sponsor or a trustworthy person instead of dwelling in the labyrinth of my mind. Most importantly, I found a way to connect with God, and to stay connected. I discovered that helping others is the key to maintaining that connection. I finally found my calling and purpose in life. All this time, I had been trying to treat a spiritual malady with non-spiritual solutions. But I found I could only treat a spiritual malady with true spirituality and a connection to a God of my own understanding.

I can't say I follow these principles perfectly, but every day, one day at a time, I do my best with the help of God and my fellows. Today, I live a life I am proud of. I embrace discomfort because I know it is a gift from God and an opportunity to grow. I have a job that lets me help other people. I am active in the fellowship of Heroin Anonymous and embrace the newcomer just as I was once embraced. I do my best to be a beacon of bright light to help others. I sponsor men through the steps just as I was sponsored and taught how to live by these spiritual principles. Those men are now sponsoring others. I also do service work for Heroin Anonymous on the regional level.

Today, I have a college degree and a loving girlfriend who accepts me for my past and present, and I hold many non-transactional friendships dearly in my heart. I have accomplished things today that I would have never been able to achieve without the spiritual principles of this program. All of these accomplishments are great, but most of all, I have God. I finally have serenity, that ease and comfort I had always been searching for. All this time, it was within me. I hope you can find it, too.

MY SISTER AND ME

Heroin Anonymous helped her cope with her emotions and fears. Recovery doesn't have to be linear!

Even when I was a child, I never felt at ease. Everything just felt too overwhelming. I don't remember a lot from back then. I know now my parents did the best they could, and I know I didn't give them much to work with. I attempted suicide for the first time at the age of 10. For as long as I had a consciousness of life, I resented it. I didn't fit in, and my feelings were so big and out of control that I would lash out. I was constantly seeking relief. Even when I snuck downstairs as a child and grabbed the biggest kitchen knife I could find to hold against my belly, I was seeking relief from the anguish between my ears. I wanted it to end, and I thought the only way to stop it was to cut it out from the source.

I scared myself so much that I woke up my

mom and told her what had happened. She held me all night on the couch and cried with me. How could a child have so much pain that they would be pushed to such extremes? My journey of seeking was just beginning. The truth is, I never thought my life would have any worth. It wasn't until I did the work and reached the Ninth Step that the promises started to come true for me. I now see that "no matter how far down the scale we have gone, we will see how our experience can benefit others." Today, my sobriety is the most precious thing in the world. Without it, I am beyond human aid. I am in the grips of my defects; I am cut off from the source.

I started seeing mental health professionals soon after the kitchen knife incident. For a long time, I resented my parents for paying someone to do their job. I thought the professionals were the biggest frauds of all. Pretending to care about me for money – what could be worse than that? I learned something else from my first suicide attempt. I had found relief in the love and comfort my mother gave me that night, and so I learned that being in distress was a good way to get attention and love from others. It was the beginning of a victim mentality. I was constantly seeking comfort, anything to relieve the war inside my heart.

I had my first drink at the age of 12 or 13. I was at an ice skating rink with the cool kids, and I felt honored just to be in their presence. Someone passed around a soda bottle filled with alcohol from their parents' liquor cabinet. Immediately after the first sip, I needed more. I couldn't get enough. I got hammered that night, and my friend's mother, who drove us home, knew I was drunk and told my parents. That night, I swallowed a whole bunch of headache medicine to kill myself. I threw up almost immediately and then went to bed. The insanity of addiction struck me very quickly. From then on, I became friends with anyone who drank and would do it as often as I could. I regularly brought alcohol to school. I felt alive for the first time in my life.

When I was 16, I went to a party and met the girl who would become my best friend – my sister. Right away, we were inseparable. At that same party, someone offered us a line of something. At this point, I had already done acid, molly, cocaine, ecstasy, and anything else I could get my hands on. So, when this stranger offered us a line, I didn't think twice. Immediately, I knew this substance was like nothing I had ever done before. I asked what it was, and he told me it was heroin. The peace and comfort that washed over me drowned out any voices of rationality. I should have stopped and asked myself, "You're 16, and you just did *heroin*. What is wrong with you?" Instead, I asked the only question I ever asked from then on, "Do you have more?"

My memory of that night is very foggy. I just know that I had finally found my salvation, along with a new best friend. I had been saved, and my savior's name was Heroin. "I met God and the Devil tonight" is what I wrote in my diary. I knew in my heart that something that made me feel this good must be evil. A wolf in sheep's clothing. Imprisonment through the delusion of freedom. But I also knew I would chase this high to the ends of the earth. My whole life became fixated on how to get the next high.

I changed crowds again and started spending as much time as I could with my new best friend and the guy who gave us that first line. My other party friends were still content with doing cocaine, drinking, and hallucinating once in a while on shriveled-up mushrooms, but my new sister and I needed something more. I tried to keep my heroin use a secret, but soon everyone would know that I was addicted and had no plans of stopping.

I experienced consequences from my use

almost as soon as I started. The first time I drove a car at night by myself, I was pulled over and charged with a DUI, but I didn't think I had a problem. I was caught in school multiple times with pills, alcohol, cigarettes, and weed, but I was never expelled. I would be given detention, and even when they found drugs, the principal had a hall monitor throw them out in the dumpster so they didn't have to call the police on me. I would have lunch with the principal and ask him for money for food, saying I had none at home. I would take his money and buy drugs with it. So many people wanted to help me. I just couldn't see that I needed it. I had only one mission: to escape myself as fast as I could.

My new friends started dying of overdoses, suicide, and car accidents. We would gather at someone's house and get high before the funeral. I felt like I finally had a family that understood me. I received so much love and attention for the grief I was experiencing. It only enhanced the victim mentality I wore like armor. It felt as though I got a free pass to do whatever I wanted because everyone felt so bad for me. I ate it up.

After years of using together, my new best friend decided she wanted to be sober. I was happy for her. She asked me to go to a 12-Step meeting with her. At the meeting, I stood up awkwardly and said, "I'm here to support my friend. I'm so glad you guys have each other." I was in a room full of people who used like me and had found a way out, but I wasn't looking for an exit. I became skeptical of the program as soon as my friend started talking to me about God. I was terrified that the rooms were taking her weaknesses and exploiting them to convert her to organized religion. She told me God can be anything she chooses, as long as it's not her or another human being. The truth is, I was more afraid of her finding God and changing than I was of her using heroin again. That's how delusional I was. I was so wrapped up in myself and focused on getting high that I didn't even notice when my friend relapsed.

The day she died from an overdose, I reached a depth I didn't think possible. People say certain substances or situations brought them into the rooms. For me, it was grief. The grief that followed my friend's passing threw me into a drug and alcohol-induced frenzy. I came undone. I was unhinged, and no one was safe. It was as if my soul snapped. A part of me died, and it had to die in order for me to be here today. At the funeral, her brother held me and said, "I'm not the only one who lost a sister today." I owe my sobriety and my life to my friend and her passing.

For three years, I put whatever substance I could into my body to avoid reality. I couldn't stomach the thought of a world without my friend in it. I would stay in my room all day, using and going in and out of consciousness. I attempted suicide again and again. My world became so small. It was only me and my drugs, and anything that got in our way became a casualty.

I truly believe that if I hadn't hit such a dark bottom, I would not be alive today. I have seen the depths of hell. I have walked through the valley of the shadow of death, desperate for relief.

One day, out of nowhere, something dawned on me. Maybe a spiritual retreat could bring relief to the pain I carried. I searched for retreats, getaways, and vacations. Then, my Higher Power did for me what I could not do for myself. For the first time in my life, the thought of rehab entered my mind. I called and spoke to someone at a nearby treatment facility. As I detoxed alone in my bedroom, the facility sent a car to pick me up.

I spent 28 days in inpatient treatment, and I compared myself to the other women there the whole time. I wasn't as bad as these people. Sure,

I was addicted to heroin, but I never used the needle, and I never went to the physical depths some of these people went to. Was I really a bad enough user to deserve a way out?

My sobriety was off and on for a while, and a lot happened to me in early recovery. Eight months into my newfound sobriety, I found my boyfriend dead of an overdose. I came to believe that anyone who got too close to me would die. Anything I touched would rot. I held so much guilt and shame because I thought I had the power to save and kill people. I stayed sober until I didn't, and then I would come back into the rooms and try again.

At the time, I attended an alcohol-focused program because Heroin Anonymous hadn't yet arrived in my state. Once it did, I played the comparison game again. Someone even told me that I didn't belong in H.A. because I didn't use the needle like them. I was full of despair, thinking, "I'm not even good enough to be accepted by junkies." I kept coming back, though. Something in me told me this was my home. I knew I was an alcoholic; that was clear as day. What wasn't so clear was whether I belonged in this room full of heroin addicts just because I didn't use exactly how most of them used. I loved pills and putting heroin up my nose, but I never used the needle.

I finally put together four years of continuous sobriety. I had gone through multiple sponsors. I would eventually stop calling them, and once they told me I needed to work harder, I would find a new sponsor. I got up to the Fourth Step repeatedly but would always stall out of fear of telling someone all of my secrets.

In time, the obsession to drink left me, but the obsession to use opiates remained. I thought if I could just relapse and use the needle, I would finally fit in and be accepted. The dangers of feeling excluded can be life or death. I fell back into bad habits, and slowly but surely, I pulled away from what little program I had left. Eight months before I relapsed, I stole pills from my aunt. I held on to them for months, telling myself, "Look, I'm not an addict anymore. I can hold onto these pills and not use them." The issue was that I couldn't get rid of them either.

I used for the last time in 2021. I was dog-sitting in a beautiful mansion with a full bar. I had hit a bottom unlike any other I had experienced while using, but I was dead-sober. And dead sober I was. The mental obsession took over, and I walked to the bar, poured a shot, and swallowed it. It was on. I couldn't stop taking shots. I remembered I had the pills in my car, just in case of emergency, and this was the emergency. I snorted all of the pills and drank until I passed out. I somehow woke up the next morning with incomprehensible demoralization.

My whole life changed after that relapse. I came back to the rooms of Heroin Anonymous, ready to take any suggestions and willing to go to any lengths to never feel that way again, especially sober. I hit bottom in sobriety because I didn't have a solution. I thought simply not using would be enough to lead a life of happiness, but I was wrong. The substance use was just a symptom of my disease, and if I fall into the trap of thinking that heroin and alcohol are my problem, I will die.

Back in the rooms of Heroin Anonymous, I began to join committees and do service. I started to share at meetings and tell the truth about what was really going on. I had finally accepted my story and was no longer ashamed that I didn't use the exact way many of my peers did. I was home.

Through the most painful experiences, I was pushed into a far better life. I learned that if I just hold on, don't use, and do the next right thing, even through the most trying times, I would be rocketed into the fourth dimension. What I came to realize was that I *did* belong in H.A.

from the beginning. My addiction wanted me to think otherwise because it wasn't done with me. It will never be done with me. It will find ways to infiltrate my thoughts and make me feel apart from others in any circumstance.

I learned that when I share, when I do service, and when I share my experience, strength, and hope, I move past my pain. I have recovered from a hopeless state of mind, body, and spirit. I believe I will always be an addict and alcoholic, and I will always need this program to live a long and prosperous life. Today, I don't use, no matter what.

I found that the only way to get more out of my sobriety was to be willing to give absolutely all of it away to the next sick and suffering heroin addict. I also learned that I can't determine who that will be. I suffered from a savior complex for many years, and it still flares up if I don't keep in fit spiritual condition. I would pick and choose who I would help and who needed it the most.

Today, I know that as long as I keep speaking and sharing my pain and my hope, the right person will hear it. Even if that someone is me. I need to hear my story over and over again to keep it fresh in my mind. I can't forget that there is always another bottom out there waiting for me.

However, I'm not sure if there's another recovery.

I found a home in Heroin Anonymous. I embrace all sides of the triangle today – unity, service, and recovery. I make sure I have unity with the fellowship by attending events and fellowshipping before and after the meeting. I do service by sponsoring, making coffee, greeting my fellows, or chairing meetings. I go through the steps periodically to ensure recovery is in my life at all times. I give back and pay it forward by talking to the newcomer.

My journey of healing has not been linear. There have been many setbacks. I know that there is no such thing as perfection. If we could be perfect, we wouldn't need God. And, boy, do I need God.

Today, I live a life beyond my wildest dreams. I would have settled for not using and not wanting to die every day. I would have settled for a life not run by drugs and alcohol. What I received instead was joy, friendship, peace, and serenity. I get to keep these and more by being willing to give them all away to the next sick and suffering addict.

That's why the newcomer is the most important person in the room. It is my life's purpose to ensure they know that there is a way out, so long as they follow a few simple steps.

I TOLD ON MYSELF

*Both of her parents were in recovery. Once
she found a Higher Power of her own
understanding, the door opened for her, too.*

I'm a 12-Step baby. My parents married
while in recovery together, had three kids, then
divorced. My earliest memories are the love I
had for my mishmash family, coupled with the
devastating pain I felt after my parents got re-
divorced. I was a confused-yet-capable, attention-
starved little girl, always hopelessly yearning for
validation.

When I was a little older, I embraced my
life as the party girl, smoking weed every day
and drinking as much as I wanted. I thought I
was thriving; I could be as loud and funny as I
wanted to be. Alcohol and marijuana progressed
to cocaine and party drugs. My parents could
tell I was an alcoholic before I ever took a legal

drink, but I laughed them off. I wasn't like them. It wasn't until I snorted my first painkiller that I started to wonder if they were right. Within a month, I was physically addicted. Within six months, I was selling and robbing to sustain the addiction. Within a year, I had switched from pills to heroin. I didn't know what was in that blue stamp; frankly, I didn't care. I was now shackled to the bag and the block.

I somehow managed to graduate from college and get a big girl job. I "successfully" lived a double life until the fear of dying an addict's death on skid row finally outweighed the fear of dopesickness. So, when the opportunity presented itself, I ran. I didn't say goodbye to my family or call out of work. I just ran. I detoxed cold turkey during a cross-country drive from my East Coast hometown to the desert out West. The palm trees and sunshine felt like a fresh start. The heroin was out of my system, but there was nothing to take its place. The cycle restarted. Alcohol and marijuana again progressed to cocaine and party drugs, but I promised myself I would never do heroin again.

One Saturday night in October, I was preparing for the festivities of the night, rolling a blunt and drinking a tall can of light beer. What I didn't know was that this night would be the start of a journey that led me to my true spiritual bottom, and shortly thereafter, recovery. That night, I got a call and was asked to go check on my aunt, who lived nearby. Since leaving home, I've gotten the opportunity to build a new relationship with her. She had helped raise me for as long as I could remember, but now I was grown up, and she trusted me with her spare key and even gave me work when I was broke. But when I got to her home, she had passed away. There was nothing I could do. Death was so real and so close. From that moment, I began to knowingly drink for oblivion. I didn't want to die, but I definitely didn't want to live. After a weekend of partying and binging, I finally had an honest moment with myself: I knew it was only a matter of time until I broke the promise I made myself. I was going to do heroin again. I've had lots of these moments where I knew I was going to die but did nothing about it. But this time was different; I didn't want my sister to find me dead like I had just found my aunt. So, before I gave myself the opportunity to use opiates again, I told on myself. "I'm a heroin addict. I'm terrified of myself."

I went to a meeting and found a sponsor quickly. With her guidance, I found myself in the book *Alcoholics Anonymous*. It was easy for me to admit I was powerless over heroin; who can do heroin recreationally? The profound realization was this: The first drink will lead me to my one true love (heroin) and, inevitably, death. I can't just change the substance I'm using; I need to change the thoughts and beliefs behind my need to use in the first place.

For someone as violently anti-religious as I was, the "We Agnostics" chapter in the Big Book was hard to argue with. I had abandoned any idea of God. But other times, I would be absorbed in contemplation of the cosmos (and aliens), usually high out of my mind, and wonder, "Who, then, made all this?" That feeling of awe and wonder was often fleeting, passing in and out of my brain so quickly. But this book was telling me that I only had to grasp onto that feeling for recovery to be possible. I could definitely do that.

When I came to H.A., I genuinely considered myself to be an honest person. My 4th and 5th Steps showed me how wrong I was. I had been blatantly lying to everyone around me for years. It was hard to deny any of my character defects after realizing the hypocrisy of my life as I had been living it. The light shining on my ego was so bright it felt like I was burning. But by the time I made amends both to those closest to me and to those I had been avoiding, the wounds healed into scars. The steps put an end to my double life, and I could finally feel whole.

Staying sober while practicing Steps 10, 11, and 12 is how I make amends to myself every day. Through prayer and meditation, I keep working to improve my understanding of and relationship with God, which allows me to go out into the world as a changed human being and help whoever God puts in my path. It's not rocket science.

Without a doubt, my main passion in H.A. is service with the hospitals and institutions committee. Through my H&I work, I help bring meetings to addicts confined to hospitals and other institutions, like so many addicts and alcoholics before me. There are thousands of treatment and correction centers full of addicts, and I'm so glad H.A. has committees to help carry the message of recovery into as many of those facilities as possible. It's the greatest privilege to be a part of this.

I've found a home in H.A. that I never wanted. Here, I can share my love for the book *Alcoholics Anonymous* while also sharing my experience as a dope fiend. I'm uniquely qualified to help heroin addicts identify with a book published back in 1939, long before our current opioid epidemic was even fathomable. Not only are hundreds of my fellows dropping into oblivion around me all the time, but hundreds of my fellows are dying every single day.[1] I am spared this fate on a daily basis, and therefore I direct my thoughts and actions to sharing the gift of recovery with one more addict, God willing.

---

1. As of 2023, an average of 217 people died every day from an opioid overdose in the United States, according to the U.S. Centers for Disease Control and Prevention.

FILLING THE VOID
IN MY HEART

*She tried heroin, stripping, and transactional
relationships to heal her heart. H.A.
provided the love she truly needed.*

My early life was filled with love thanks to
my grandparents. They provided structure and
everything else I needed to grow up into a well-
rounded person. They also kept me safe and
protected me from my dysfunctional mother. She
wasn't interested in me anyway, so it worked out.
She loved getting high and partying. I watched
her get locked up constantly and go in and out
of treatment for her pill addiction. This should
have been a deterrent, but drugs drew me in by
the time I was 12.

When I went to live with my mom, I knew
that I wasn't being smart, but I was getting bored
with Grandma and Grandpa. Right away, my

spiritual malady started to really rock me. Mom and I immediately started getting high together. We finally had a connection. I felt her approval when I came home from my doctor's appointment with a prescription for opioid pain pills. When we shared them, I felt the warm sense of ease and comfort I had been looking for my whole life. I felt loved.

I ended up having two children at a young age and was a single mother by 19. I neglected them, and they were occasionally taken away to Grandma's to be looked after. Drugs took over my love for them, and I was always trying to pawn them off on anyone who would take them. I loved my kids, but I was chasing that warm opiate high, stuck in a delusion that I was a better mom when I was high. The day came when Child Protective Services was called, and they removed my kids from my care. I swore I would get sober for real and go to treatment. So, I reluctantly went to a 28-day program.

To my surprise, I loved treatment and thought I was cured. The day I got out, I was excitedly walking to a 12-Step meeting – and went right into a bar instead. A man at the bar handed me a tinfoil pack of dope. I took it, ran to the bathroom, and sat on the toilet. Here, I evaluated my choices:

do the dope or lose my kids. I was rocked by a peculiar mental twist and had zero defense against it, so I chose the dope. Sure enough, my kids were immediately removed from my care the next day. The court terminated my parental rights without a second chance. The pain of losing my kids for good was unlike anything I have ever felt, and the only relief came from getting high. Heroin took them away from me, and it was also the only thing that helped me feel better. I cried for months in my room, all alone. I loved my children and could not understand why I chose drugs over them.

I still hung out in a 12-Step fellowship for a while, but soon I was ready for a new adventure. One night, some members of the group who weren't quite recovered went out to a local strip club. The club had lost its liquor license for serving minors, and we figured it was a safe place for us to chill. As it turns out, this was not a good idea. At the end of the night, they left, and I stayed to work. My new life dancing seemed like the solution. I found a place where I could do drugs and drink with impunity. In fact, it was encouraged. I got paid to party, and it was a blast. I learned the pole tricks, bought the sexy outfits, and formed relationships with the other dancers. I had arrived.

Manipulating men for money and destroying families started weighing on my conscience, and the drugs I was doing weren't blotting it out anymore. That is, until a dancer came in with heroin. She gave me some, I shot it up, and I immediately felt that warm flush of love. It was like nothing I'd ever felt before. Heroin did for me what I could not do for myself. It took me to the place I was looking for my entire life. Soon after, my mother died of a fentanyl overdose, and I started using heroin nonstop. I ended up meeting a nice, normal man at the club who started taking care of me. I was prostituting behind his back to get $300 a day, enough to buy heroin.

I wasn't even getting high anymore; I was just trying to get well. The withdrawal I felt coming off heroin was so painful, and all the horrible things that ever happened to me would resurface and put me into the worst depression. The only solution was to find more heroin. If this is what sobriety felt like, then I didn't want anything to do with it. With my mom dead and my kids gone, it felt like I had nothing left to live for anyway, so I may as well send it all the way to the grave, I thought.

One day, I started to feel a bit off, so I took a pregnancy test. It was positive, and I was devastated. I did not want to lose another child to my heroin addiction, but I didn't see a way out. I let the nice normie guy know that he was probably the father, and he tried his best to help me. I ended up nodding off in a casino parking lot and getting arrested. I was put on medication-assisted treatment (MAT) and made to sit my entire pregnancy in jail. I didn't mind jail too much because I had a chemical solution, commissary funds, and some nice ladies from Alcoholics Anonymous were bringing in the message of the Big Book.

The day I gave birth, I was released. I now had a beautiful baby girl with a man who truly cared about me. Unlike my other kids' dads, he wanted to help and change diapers. I had everything I ever wanted. Surely, they would be enough to keep me sober. Then, when my daughter was 3 months old, the phenomenon of craving cranked up, and suddenly I needed more than just MAT. I started doing meth and spun out of control very quickly. My good doctor saw what a mess I was, and he called CPS on me. Once again, my baby was taken away, not only from me, but from her dad as well. This scared him enough to kick me out, and I was left to couch surf for a couple months.

One day, I was scrolling through social media looking for a way out, and I stumbled upon a treatment center in Southern California that advertised holistic treatment options like hot stones, dialectical behavior therapy (DBT), and acupuncture. This seemed like the kind of place I could get sober, even though I had already been in four treatment centers (and seven jail stays). The only problem was they wouldn't accept my state aid insurance, so I begged my boyfriend to marry me so I could get on his good health insurance. He very reluctantly agreed, and we got married. A few days later, I got on a plane and soon arrived at a million-dollar mansion overlooking the Pacific Ocean. Inside, I saw a Big Book on the table, and I was not happy about that at first.

As I lay in the detox room, I felt the old mental obsession start to take hold, and I was crying nonstop. A rehab worker came in with that Big Book in her hand and opened it to the "Doctor's Opinion" section. She read, "Frothy emotional appeal seldom suffices." She then explained to me what that actually meant. My family's begging and pleading to stop – and even wanting to stop myself – wasn't enough to get me sober. The message that could interest and hold me had to have depth and weight. Her words flew through me and I finally understood what was wrong with me. She went on to explain the two-fold nature of my illness – mental obsession and physical craving. The mental obsession drove me to relapse, then the physical craving took over, and I couldn't stop. This made sense to me, and I had a profound First Step experience.

I felt an intense sense of urgency to get a sponsor and work the steps, which is exactly what I did. I walked into my first Heroin Anonymous meeting wearing long sleeves even though it was 90 degrees outside. I was so ashamed of my track marks and always went to great lengths to hide them. But to my amazement, the other heroin addicts were all dressed like me and were comparing their old junkie wounds like it was cool or something. This blew me away! They had a certain glow about them, and they were reading out of the Big Book of Alcoholics Anonymous. Wherever it said the word alcohol, they would substitute it for heroin.

I got my first sponsor that night, and she took me through all Twelve Steps in 60 days. I wrote out my Fourth Step in one night. I did this because I literally felt like I was going to die if I didn't. This sense of urgency carried me through the program, and I started sponsoring right away. I had many profound spiritual experiences and finally felt useful, for once in my life.

When I returned home from treatment, I attended other recovery fellowships, but it wasn't the same. I couldn't relate to them and felt a void in my heart, missing Heroin Anonymous.

One day, I saw a flier for an H.A. meeting in a town an hour south from my house. When I went to the meeting, the chair gave me a stack of Big Books and a meeting start-up kit, so I went home and started H.A. in my area. This was difficult because I got a lot of backlash from members of another fellowship, and I lost a lot of friends because of it. I did not care though; the Big Book tells us that God will help us build the fellowship we crave, and He did just that.

We soon started a local H.A. meeting in our jail, and people started funneling into the rooms through that. It grew into six meetings a week, and now we have our own district and sent a delegate to the latest H.A. conference. Watching other suffering heroin addicts find a solution will always be the bright spot in my life. This is what I was meant to do in life – to carry the message.

Heroin Anonymous brought my children back to me. I am employable again. I show up where and when I say I am going to.

Today, I enjoy the warm rush of God's love

and the ability to give back what was so freely given to me, and I am forever grateful for this beautiful fellowship.

DEAD ON ARRIVAL

He expected to die by the needle and spoon.
By the grace of a Higher Power, he found
a life of peace in sobriety instead.

I was born in a large city in California, and I was raised in a middle-class town, in a middle-class family, and in a middle-class home. My grades were good, I played honors violin, and I went on trips with my parents. The first eight years of my life were happy, but looking back, I'm not sure my parents were really ready for the responsibility of raising a child.

When my dad went on a trip to Europe with a female coworker, my family quickly fell into shambles. My father cheated first, then my mother cheated with his boss, and before I knew it, they were living in separate houses. My mother tried to continue to be a good parent, but children of divorce often have abandonment issues, and I certainly did after their whirlwind divorce. My father's endless resentment toward my mother only made these problems worse, and soon I began to believe my mom was to blame for my broken family, and I took on those resentments at a young age. I was so angry.

While this was happening, my only friend in the world introduced me to weed and self-harm. As my family fell apart, I hid out at my friend's house, getting stoned and watching movies. I loved this feeling, and it was a welcome distraction from the chaos at home. My grades began to slip, and within a few years, I started to experience serious depression. I became increasingly antisocial, and around seventh grade, I moved in with Dad. He wanted to be my friend, and most importantly, he turned a blind eye to my drug use and had no qualms when I decided to grow pot and sell drugs.

During these years, I came to believe that there had to be a chemical solution to my depression. I needed some chemical peace of mind to soothe my thoughts of suicide. Something that could fill what I now know is the God-sized hole inside me. So, I began to search for other drugs. In my case, the progression was quick, and I went from pothead to psychedelic-head to meth-head.

As I was escaping into drugs, my home

life became even more chaotic. Dad filled the 4-bedroom home he got in the divorce with sketchy roommates he found online. So, I put a loveseat in the garage and took it for my bedroom. I loved it – I sold drugs and partied with the roommates, and I was able to use the garage as a home base for my chief occupation, selling drugs to stay high.

My father was and has always been a militant atheist, and this was one of the biggest beliefs I picked up from him. In my mind, God couldn't exist because my life was so terrible, but keeping that mentality was always an uphill battle. Having no faith takes a lot more effort than having just a little. Between the drugs, the dealing, and the existential crises, I wasn't doing great.

By the time I started high school, I was smoking and selling meth. In my freshman year, I missed all but a week of the first semester, so the principal called in both of my parents to let them know I was being expelled and pointed me in the direction of a psychiatric institution for help. Thinking that I would just see a psychiatrist, Mom brought me in, but after seeing the self-inflicted cuts on my arms and the burns on my hands, I was institutionalized for the first time. I was held for 72 hours, and the experience was traumatic for my

14-year-old self. When I got out, I turned to the only friend I had – drugs.

Shortly after this experience, painkillers came into my life and changed it for the worse. It was the oxy era, and in painkillers, I finally found the peace of mind I had been searching for all those years. I dived in headfirst. Unfortunately for me, the oxy wave was on its way out almost as soon as I got in, and when the well dried up six months later, heroin rushed in to fill the market.

Heroin became the first and last thing on my mind every day. And as those days turned to weeks and months, it became harder and harder for Dad to turn a blind eye to my drug use. When he invited me to my cousin's wedding on the other side of the country, I knew we'd be driving for days just to get there. I did the math, and I thought six grams would be enough to get me through the whole event. It was not. By the time we arrived, I was already going through withdrawal, and on the day of the wedding, I stole the spotlight, made a fool of myself, and flew home with my tail tucked between my legs.

Shortly thereafter, Dad kicked me out, and I fell back on the only people I could think of – my customers. After all, they relied on me to get their fix.

Not long after losing my garage home, I began to have run-ins with the police. In 2019, I caught back-to-back felony sales charges for the first time, and I was sentenced to three months in jail and three months in a treatment program. This program was the first experience I had with the radical idea that you could be both sober and not miserable. I learned about the Twelve Steps of Alcoholics Anonymous, even if I was not yet prepared to work the steps myself. For 90 days, day in and day out, I had the Big Book spoon-fed to me in easily digestible, bite-sized chunks. They drilled the Big Book into my head so hard that even years later I could still recite the 9th-Step promises from memory.

I was 19 years old, and I thought, "This place is a cult for people who want to be sheep. I don't need a crutch named God." I didn't see the irony in that kind of thinking. I wasn't ready to embrace the concept of being powerless over drugs, but I was willing to play the part if it meant not going right back to jail.

I graduated from that program, but because I didn't implement any of the principles I had learned, my life quickly deteriorated. It didn't take long before I was back in a jail cell for a probation violation. By the time I got out, fentanyl had just hit the streets, and having no place to go, I moved in with a girlfriend.

Our relationship was incredibly toxic, and after getting into an argument, I bought a dime bag from the dealer who was living in the other room. Thinking it was heroin, I had no problem shooting it, but as soon as I did, I lost consciousness. I had to get Narcanned repeatedly over the course of 30 minutes before I came to. The kicker was that when a friend overdosed six hours later, there was no Narcan left, and he died. I tried everything I could think of to bring him back, but nothing worked, and he was ultimately dead on arrival when I brought him to the hospital. I could have called 911, but my self-centeredness and my fear of returning to jail stopped me. These are the consequences of self-will run riot.

I thought about that day all the time. Why did God keep me and let him go? The shock of my friend's death genuinely brought God back into my conscious thought, and while I still felt uneasy about God, He was once again renting space in my head. However, even this event wasn't enough for me to sober up, and a few months later, the DEA knocked on our door. I was sent to jail for another sales case. Even while locked up, I didn't stay sober for long, and by the time I got out, I had no intention of wasting time with sobriety. So, the very night I was released, I watched another friend die of a fentanyl overdose. I tried performing CPR, but it wasn't working, and when I heard sirens, I ran.

I hated fentanyl by that point – it had taken two of my friends and almost killed me – but that didn't stop me from getting high and selling it. That's the insanity of the disease and the mental obsession. If a substance could fill that God-sized hole for even a second, I couldn't stop myself.

The consequences of my addiction continued to get worse. It always gets worse. I suffered the loss of friends, alienation from my family, homelessness, and jail, but it didn't matter.

I spent the next three years using fentanyl to numb the trauma and selling it to survive. In my last and final drug case, my hotel room was raided, and I was charged for having an illegal firearm and selling fentanyl and meth.

I was facing a litany of charges and seven years in prison. I had nothing but empty relationships with empty people, and I was so tired, but I didn't know any other way to live. Given the choice between prison or treatment and probation, I decided to once again fake my way through treatment. If necessary, I would go on the run until they caught me. Instead, something incredible happened.

While I was waiting to check into rehab, I spent a few days getting high in my car. I woke up from a nod and had my first truly spiritual experience. I felt it was time to finally try sobriety. From the outside looking in, it might not sound spiritual at all, but for an addict like me, who expected to live and die by the needle and spoon, it was a profound moment. For the first time, I believed I could find peace in sobriety, and so I held onto that feeling and ran with it.

As soon as I got through detox and got my phone back, I found a sponsor and began working the 12 Steps. In the first month and a half, I did the first 10 Steps and ran a program like my life depended on it, because it absolutely did.

By chance, at a random meeting about an hour away from my program, I heard someone qualify, someone whose sobriety and recovery I wanted. So, I asked them to be my sponsor and started back at the 1st Step. By the time I graduated from the program, something had inexplicably changed in me. I used to fight the very idea of a Higher Power, but now I was praying every day. I held grudges and resentments against so many people in my life, but I learned how many of these resentments were my own doing, and no one else's. Most importantly, I was no longer trying to run the show, and my life flowed with positivity.

Through the process of working the steps, I began repairing relationships with those same family members I once screwed over and ghosted. Through an amends, my mother opened her door to me and allowed me the time I needed to get back on my feet. My father was still bitter and full of resentment, but I no longer held onto that bitterness like it was my own and was finally able to love him for who he is. I no longer resent him for who he isn't.

By chance, while looking for a meeting one night, I walked into the same H.A. meeting I once went to while loaded seven years prior. I knew right away I had found a room of like-minded addicts who I could relate to. The messages I heard and the recovery I felt in the room were powerful, so I stuck around. With six months sober, I began to look for other meetings in our fellowship, and I saw there was a need in my hometown, where no H.A. existed. I wanted to bring H.A. to more people, so I started a meeting. Through this process, my recovery blossomed. By being of service and bringing the message of Heroin Anonymous to my home, I became exponentially more plugged into my community. I even got the opportunity to bring an H.A. meeting to a detox program, where I can share the experience, strength, and hope of our community with those who want a better way of life.

Today, my relationships are no longer *quid pro quo*. I can rely on the people around me for support without wondering what they want in return. Today, that God-sized hole inside me is finally full. My relationship with my Higher Power is ever-changing, but it is strong.

The Twelve Steps, the Big Book, and the fellowship of Heroin Anonymous have given me a life of substance, a life worth living. I have a good job that allows me to help people. I can use my experiences with death, hopelessness, and a broken home to help the next man or woman seeking recovery from heroin and fentanyl.

The material things I have now – the house, the car, the girlfriend – are all byproducts of living a spiritual life. But whether I have those things or not, I know that I'm going to be okay. I can handle life on life's terms without having to turn to a needle to make it better.

Through God and this program, I have found

the peace of mind I spent 13 years searching for
with drugs. The least I can do is pass on this gift
to the next addict who wants it.

GET SHOCKED

*This heroin user crossed the line from
recreational use to addiction. He had to
choose: change his perspective or die.*

Growing up in a household with a drug-dealing, pain pill-addicted father exposed me to things that kids shouldn't see. I remember watching the foot traffic of people coming and going from our apartment and how happy a lot of them were to see my dad. I also remember the dark times, like when my dad put a pistol to a guy's head on our front stoop. I didn't fully understand the gravity of my childhood environment until my teenage years, when I started to mimic some of what I had seen as a kid. My behavior disturbed those around me, but I was totally comfortable with a drug addict lifestyle.

My father was a charming man who usually worked but sold drugs on the side to make ends meet. He was a master manipulator and constantly played the victim. I remember him telling sad stories about his childhood and all of the bad things that he had been through. I heard them so often that I have the stories memorized. I also remember noticing how easily he convinced people to do things for him after he told them his sad stories.

My mother did the best she could amidst a chaotic situation, but she taught me to lie to others about the things I was seeing at home, which resulted in me forming a habit of lying whenever it was slightly convenient for me to do so. I had one sibling: a brother who was 18 months younger than me. My little brother was a combination of the worst parts of my two parents and became an uncontrollable drug addict by the time he was 12 years old. He was so wild and crazy that he did a couple of years in a juvenile detention center. I was able to fly under the radar for most of the trouble I caused as a kid because my brother's behavior was so ridiculous that it drew a lot of attention.

I don't think that childhood trauma is a requirement for becoming a heroin addict, but I know that many of us experienced it, and I certainly did.

I didn't immediately become a heroin addict. I attended private, Catholic schools for most of my life and always did well in school. My drug career began at 14 when I smoked weed with my younger brother. It quickly progressed, getting more serious and dark over a decade and a half. I realized that I had a set of traits that suited me well to be a drug addict – I knew how to manipulate people by playing the victim and constantly lied when it helped me to get what I wanted, which was more drugs. It didn't take long for my drug use to become problematic and affect my personal relationships. Several of my Catholic school teenage friends approached me, expressing concern for my near-constant intoxication. My response to them was always some version of, "If you had been through what I have been through, then you would be doing this too." None of my private school friend group had the chaotic home life that I had, so they would agree with my reasoning and back off.

There was one person, however, who told me something so profound that it has stuck with me until this day. After hearing my sad story spiel, she said that she was sorry that I had experienced those things, but then she asked me a question. She asked, "At what point does it stop being something that happened to you and start becoming something that you choose?" Even now, with over a decade sober, I still don't know the exact answer to that question, but I believe at some point all of us in the "childhood trauma club" cross an invisible line where it starts becoming something that we choose. Certainly, I was set on a path in life due to the things that I experienced as a child. At times, these experiences made it very comfortable for me to walk down the drug path. Yet, at some point, I chose to continue to walk down that path. Later in life, I would reflect on what my friend said and would come to realize that sustained sobriety was impossible for me until I escaped the victimhood mentality. I find a lot of truth in that old saying, "victims don't get better." If I am the victim, then I lack the power to do anything to change for the better. I had to learn to become accountable for my actions, and when I did, I inadvertently gained the power to change. I had to escape the vicious cycle of playing the victim card to avoid accountability for my poor behaviors. I think this is one of the reasons why we make such a big deal out of resentments in recovery programs – because the temptation to justify our poor behaviors as a reaction to victimization is so strong.

My home life had gotten so bad during my teenage years that I left the house and moved in with my then-girlfriend at 16. I sobered up and finished high school. As my teenage brain processed my childhood home life, disgust was my initial reaction to the chaos that I had endured living with my addict father and brother. I wanted nothing to do with them and wanted to be nothing like them. I quit drinking and doing drugs cold turkey, graduated high school, and then started college.

As a college student, I longed to have a bond with my father and brother. The two of them were close through using drugs together. I sought them out, and the three of us grew close while we drank and did drugs together during our free time. I finally had the relationship with my father and brother that I always wanted! Their drug habits were more advanced than mine. They were full-blown heroin addicts, and my father seemed to have a never-ending supply of painkillers. I limited my use of opioids during my college years and didn't inject anything or use intravenously because I witnessed what it did to my family members, and it terrified me.

Still, getting drunk and high during college caused some problems and inconveniences for me. I remember having to switch college majors because my brain couldn't do math or memorize as well as it used to once I started smoking weed every day. I switched from pre-med biology to pre-law philosophy because I could write philosophy papers and essays while high.

After college, I started law school. My opioid use started with prescribed pain pills, then pain pills I bought off the street, then snorting heroin, then injecting heroin intravenously. Before I graduated law school, heroin injections multiple times a day were required for me to function and study for the bar examination. The bar exam is split into sections over several days with breaks in between each section. I went into the bathroom stall of the bar exam testing center between sections of the test and injected heroin. I somehow passed the bar exam and began to practice law.

My little brother died at 22 from a lethal dose of opioids and benzodiazepines the week after I finished my first-year law school final exam. I blamed myself for it. My father and I were both in a very dark place. We began shooting up heroin together. We didn't know it when we first started shooting up together, but my father was in the early stages of liver failure from untreated

Hepatitis C and liver cancer. He frequently OD'd on me, and doing CPR to bring him back to life became a regular occurrence every time that we went and scored. I didn't stop shooting up, but I did stop shooting up with him. He died about a year later from liver failure.

I started to experience the problems that come with IV heroin use as I began my career working a 9-to-5 lawyer job. Drug dealers don't understand the concept of a 1-hour lunch break, and I found myself spending large amounts of time during the work day waiting in parking lots or next to abandoned buildings for them to show up with my drugs. I was spending my money on heroin faster than I could make it. I soon pawned everything of value that I owned and took out multiple payday loans. I was sometimes able to get extra money by lying and manipulating people with sad stories, just like I had watched my father do so masterfully my whole life.

IV drug use created a unique set of problems that I had never experienced before, but the most serious problem was the fact that I consistently overdosed. I would routinely fall out in the morning while doing my morning ritual and wake up on the bathroom floor hours after shooting up. This happened several times a week and would often make me late for work. The frequency of my overdoses began to concern me, but I would do it all over again the next day, like an insane person. By this point, heroin was not optional.

Sometimes I think about how insane I was while actively using heroin. I remember how excited I would get when I heard that someone had overdosed from a particularly strong batch. I would scramble up as much money as I could and race over to see which dealer had the batch that was killing people. How insane is that? I now realize how broken my brain was back then and how warped my perception of reality was. I think that you have to have a warped and delusional perception in order to maintain a heroin addiction for any meaningful amount of time because it requires a large amount of crazy to keep using heroin despite the mountain of evidence that it was destroying my life and the lives of everyone around me.

And the lies – oh, the lies! I believed so many of my own lies. Like the lie that I would quit when I was ready to quit; I just wasn't ready yet. Or that I was a better person on heroin because it helped me control my anger problem. Or that I was a more productive worker on heroin because I could sit and work for hours straight. Or that I was a better boyfriend on heroin because I could have sex longer.

I had always been able to easily quit different substances when I was ready to stop. I assumed that it would be the same way with heroin. I learned the hard way that one doesn't just stop using heroin after using daily for a period of time. The pain and misery of being dopesick was something that I couldn't imagine until I experienced it. Heroin grabbed a hold of me like no other drug had done. I gave up on detox and got high on day three or day five of being dopesick too many times to count. There really aren't adequate words to describe just how miserable being dopesick is. You either know or you don't.

I remember the panic that would set in when I ran out of heroin. Like, actual panic. I experienced calm and comfort when I still had some heroin left, but the moment it was gone, I switched into tunnel vision mode, where all I cared about was getting more. Getting more took priority over everything else. I would frequently make promises to people, but I was unable to do anything else until I did heroin first. Not having heroin was a non-starter.

I knew that being a junkie was a problem for me. I began to learn how serious the problem was when other people started finding me half-dead on the floor. During one of my overdoses, I had an out-of-body experience, watching my own body as I floated upward. I remember looking down at myself as I lay there on the bed. I kept going up and ended up in what I can best describe as the lobby of the DMV, where you sit and wait for your number to be called. It was an all-white waiting area. The lobby was crowded and filled with spirits who I didn't recognize, but with whom I felt a strong sense of connection and comfort – like family ties –my ancestors. Then, my dead father appeared to me and told me that it wasn't my time to stay there. He said it was time for me to stop living how I was living.

The next few years included multiple failed attempts to get off of heroin. The first hurdle that I overcame was to stop believing the lie that I would stop using heroin when I wanted to stop, and that I just didn't want to stop. When the day came that I realized I actually did want to stop and couldn't, a sense of panic and desperation set in. That panic and desperation eventually turned to hopelessness. I was in a very dark place, and death started to seem like a way to get some relief. Every time that I tried to stop using heroin, I not only became physically sick, but I was also emotionally crippled. I would lie in bed all day and sob, grieving the loss of my father and brother.

I realized that I required inpatient detox treatment to be able to physically separate myself from heroin after countless failed attempts to do it at home. The next hurdle that I had to overcome in my recovery journey was the mistaken belief that my heroin use had only gotten so bad because I was physically addicted to it. I thought that after I detoxed, I could go back to a life of using other drugs somewhat normally. I remember going out to a bar to have a few drinks to celebrate having 30 days off of heroin. By the end of the night, I had a bag of heroin and a needle in my arm. I was soon back to daily IV use. How did this happen?! The plan was just to have a few drinks to celebrate! Today, I know that alcohol is not for me because when my inhibitions are lowered, there is no telling what I will do while drunk. Today, I choose not to do anything if the end result might bring me back to heroin.

As I sat in my 15th or 16th medical detox center kicking heroin, I started to accept the fact that I needed to do something after I left the detox center if I wanted to stay off of heroin. There were people who came to the detox center to speak to us about the Twelve Steps of recovery.

They talked about their meetings, and I decided that I would go to one when I got out.

I remember sitting in the meeting and reading the Twelve Steps on the wall to myself. I went down the list and came up with reasons why I didn't have to do most of them. I remember disqualifying myself from the step about character defects because I honestly believed that all of my character defects were a symptom of my drug use. Now that the drugs were removed, my defects were gone. I managed to stay sober for five months one time by doing nothing but attending meetings. I have always had anger problems. At five months sober, something happened in my life, and I flew into an angry rage like I had done so many times while I was on drugs. I was shocked and disturbed that this happened because I couldn't blame the drugs this time.

I was not willing to work the steps for a long time. I couldn't make a logical connection between the steps and my drug use. I also thought that 12-Step recovery groups were unnecessary because the steps all seemed to point to God. I concluded that 12-Step groups were the equivalent of middlemen and that I would just go directly to the source. I also felt like there was some secret that I wasn't being let in on. It made me angry when they said things like, "Keep coming back. More will be revealed."

I remember angrily thinking to myself, "Why don't you just reveal it now so that I don't have to come back?!" I eventually quit going to meetings and went to church instead. I was soon back on the needle, half-dead and in another detox center.

I felt defeated. My best ideas on how to overcome my drug addiction had failed. I decided I would go to meetings, get a sponsor, and try working the steps.

I had a hard time selecting a sponsor. I spent months traveling to every meeting around, searching for someone who had the same drug of choice as me, the same Higher Power as me, and the same career as me. I finally found the guy for me. Everything was going great until he relapsed after meeting with me a few times. I didn't give up. I took his relapse as some kind of cosmic joke instead. At the next meeting I attended, I walked up to the first guy I saw and asked him to sponsor me. We met once a week and read from the Big Book. He taught me that the program of recovery was located in the Big Book and that it was an instruction manual.

I remember when we got to Step Three. I

had been preparing for weeks. Newly sober me had a big problem with Step Three. I intensely philosophized that step. I thought it was impossible for anyone to know God's will for them. I was terrified of the types of people who so confidently proclaimed to know what God's will was because they all seemed to be religious zealots and bigots. I prepared my points of discussion for weeks before I met with my sponsor to work the step.

On the day we started Step Three, I laid out my well-thought-out presentation about all of the problems with the Third Step. My sponsor politely interrupted me at some point and calmly said, "Let me ask you a few questions, and I want you to honestly answer. Maybe we can work through this." I skeptically agreed.

He asked, "Do you want to make a searching and fearless moral inventory of yourself?"

I said, "No."

He asked, "Do you want to come tell me about your inventory and admit everything on it to God?"

I said, "No."

He asked, "Do you want to identify your

character defects and try to work on them?"

I said, "No."

He asked, "Do you want to make a list of all the people you have harmed and try to go make it right?"

I said, "No."

He asked, "Do you want to keep doing inventories?"

I said, "No."

He asked, "Do you want to pray and meditate every day?"

I said, "Yes, I'll do that."

He asked, "After you do all of that, do you want to keep coming back to these meetings and telling people about it?"

I said, "Definitely not!"

He said, "Well, I just described Steps Four through Twelve to you, and you said that you didn't want to do those things, so it's not your will to do them. I will suggest to you that it's your Higher Power's will for you to do the rest of the steps." I was surprised by the simplicity of his explanation. It took someone explaining it to me like that for me to overcome the philosophical roadblocks that were preventing me from going through the process.

My sponsor did a lot of great things for me in early sobriety. He taught me how to take the lessons in the steps and apply them to my life in a meaningful way on a daily basis.

Today I understand what people mean when they say that recovery is "an inside job." It is by looking within myself during stepwork that I ultimately find and go through a spiritual awakening. Trying to put words to a spiritual experience is like trying to explain to someone what it feels like to get shocked by electricity. You're really not gonna know what I'm talking about unless you have been shocked before.

Work the Steps – get shocked. For me, the effect was electric.

CHASING GOD LIKE I CHASED DOPE

He spent time in jail, then prison. Working the Steps gave him real freedom at last.

I was born in the Upper Peninsula of Michigan and grew up in Alabama. My mother was a stay-at-home mom and my father was a tattoo artist. I remember feeling out of place and alienated. I asked a lot of big questions. Questions like, why was I here? Seeing family members drink and smoke, I didn't understand what they were doing until I went to the dentist and he put gas on my face. Then, I knew exactly what they were doing and why I was here. The drug was electric. I loved the effect, and I chased that feeling.

For the first time, I was comfortable in my own skin. I started smoking weed right after that at the age of eight. My brother was five years older than me, so I hung out with him and his friends.

I skipped school to drink, smoke weed, and use pills, later doing acid and snorting coke. I was failing all my subjects in grade school, but still got passed up to middle school.

I started tattooing like my father and making my own money at age 14. The summer of 1986 fueled my drug use as well. It seemed like I grew up really fast. I started taking school a little more seriously. After high school graduation in 1991, I went to college for one semester, then dropped out. I made more money tattooing, and school seemed like a waste of time. I started going to clubs and doing lots of ecstasy and acid and snorting powders.

At that time, I was having no real exterior problems, until I started partying in a nearby city, ran out of coke, and tried crack for the first time. This landed me on the rocks, and within six months I was in treatment for the first time. I remember they told me I would never be able to drink or use drugs successfully ever again. I questioned that.

Upon release, I did go to A.A. meetings and got a sponsor, but I did not work the program. I relapsed shortly after. For the next 20 years, I barely drew a sober breath. Running around the country from tattoo shop to tattoo shop, I thought that making geographical changes would stop my drug use, or at least slow it down, but I was wrong. I started trading medications people use for recovery (medication-assisted treatment, or MAT) for crack.

Then, I thought I found the answer: opioids. Oxy and heroin started to take center stage in my drug use. The constant chasing fueled my desire to sell crack and tattoo even more, just to keep from being sick. I did not have to search carpets anymore or stare out windows. Heroin fixed that, with it came a tidal wave of problems, like coming up with enough money to stay well. I mixed everything I could fit in a syringe.

My conscience was basically nonexistent. I got set up by a friend selling heroin. That got me six months of jail time and two years probation, with work release. I started working at a local tattoo shop, and everything went well for a while. I was using MAT during that time and had sworn off heroin, and I meant it. But in a short time, I was back using. I was baffled. I wanted to stop but couldn't. I failed UA after UA. I did jail stays.

When I finally got off paper, I thought all my problems were over. That started the worst experience of my life. I woke up to find that a friend of mine overdosed in my bathroom

– and that still wasn't enough to stop me. I started selling more and was later busted with a substantial amount of heroin. This landed me 21 months in federal prison.

While I was incarcerated, guys were carrying the message of recovery with the Big Book. I could relate to the mental obsession they were referring to. I would go back to my cell and realize I was thinking about dope for 55 minutes out of every hour. Not only had I been wrong about the God idea, but I was wrong about everything I was doing. I had been placing myself in positions to be hurt my whole life because I was always seeking more drugs in fear of running out. No wonder I was locked up. For the first time, I discovered the truth!

When I arrived at federal prison camp, I went out on the yard and saw a group of guys smoking filtered cigarettes and talking on cell phones. *Was this really prison?* I really wanted a cigarette since it had been a while. I looked at the guys across the yard and knew what the outcome would be from my past experiences. Then, an announcement came over the loudspeaker that a meeting was about to start, so I went there. This decision was completely out of my character. The guys at the meeting hooked me up with shoes, whites, and hygiene supplies.

Looking back, this was God doing for me what I could not do for myself. After that, I started seeking God like I sought out dope. This was a sufficient substitute. Within two hours of my release from prison, I was in a meeting. I got a sponsor. I started working the Twelve Steps and Traditions. I began making amends, like paying back Dad the money I swindled out of him in my crack days. In the past, I always wanted to pay him back: my intention was good, but the Power needed to carry it out wasn't there. Now, I was making a real change.

After I made a beginning, I started to experience the promises. There were a couple of H.A. meetings in my area. I took a service position with a two-year term, and I knew from that point on that H.A. was going to be my home. Eventually, I became an H.A. delegate. I started looking into the concepts and attended my first H.A. conference in Portland in 2018. I got on the Hospitals & Institutions committee, then started going to Phoenix, Arizona, looking for information on how to grow the fellowship back home.

One of our members gave me the best advice ever: to start H&I and get into the jails. That's exactly what we did, creating the fellowship that people craved. We went from two meetings a week to a meeting every night. We also take meetings into a jail for women and men. On Sunday and Tuesday, I take an H.A. meeting into the jail and explain the mental obsession and physical craving that happens in addiction. My home group has grown because it is connected to an H&I meeting. We also go into the local treatment center as well.

I found I have as much enthusiasm for the program as I did for the dope game. I sponsor other men and am disciplined on my 10th and 11th Steps. I wake up and do "On Awakening" from page 86 of the Big Book. I meditate and continue my relationship with God. I also write a nightly review that helps me keep my side of the street clean.

It seems so easy to let up on the spiritual program of action, but I know this is the treatment plan for heroin addiction, and I take it very seriously. I never miss a morning or evening meditation, and it keeps me in fit spiritual condition. I work nonstop at carrying the message to those who still suffer, especially those in jail and prison, just like it was brought to me. I get to work with a lot of men, and it is the bright spot in my life.

I am truly grateful for Heroin Anonymous. This program has definitely saved my life in more ways than one!

FOXHOLE PRAYERS

Sober since 1985, he discovered that the 12 Steps offer a solution to any and all of his problems.

Born to a middle-class New England family, alcohol was not really a mainstay in my life. My mother would stop drinking wine once she felt the effects, and I cannot remember my father ever being drunk. My older sister experimented with drugs in the Seventies but never caught the disease.

I, on the other hand, started with marijuana and whiskey at age thirteen. I smoked and drank until I passed out. If I wasn't smoking marijuana, I was thinking about it.

My family moved to London in the early Seventies, and I learned about hashish and English beer. It was a grand time to be in Swinging London. The punk and reggae scenes were just starting and the pubs never carded you.

I do remember the cop who came to my school and told us about the perils of drugs. He scared me, and I believed him. However, it didn't keep me from experimenting. By the time I was a junior in high school, I was snorting cocaine and smoking hashish every day. It didn't seem to be a problem. Everyone was getting high!

I moved back to the U.S. to go to college, and there I discovered heroin. I was scared, as I remembered what the cop had told us so many years prior. But I could prove him wrong. I snorted China white, and it was glorious. I also knew I was not addicted. We only did it every couple of weeks.

Somehow, I got through school and even got a bachelor's degree. I moved to the city and started driving a yellow cab while trying to find work in the film industry. Now, heroin was readily available. I knew I didn't have a problem, but I sure did like doing it every day. I would start my shift driving my cab "downtown" to buy some baggies of dope on the street. Mostly, the dealers took care of me, but every once and while I would get ripped off.

I noticed that I would get ill, and heroin would solve the illness. What a magical drug it was. It didn't dawn on me that I had a habit and was getting dopesick when I ran out.

I wanted to work in the film industry. A new music TV channel was in its infancy, and I really wanted to be a part of it. Besides, I heard they tolerated cocaine use. I learned that producers would even build drugs into every budget. After working there for a year, I became less and less reliable. Soon, I stopped getting called for work. With so little money available to buy dope every day, I realized I had a habit.

I wanted to quit, but I could not figure out the answer to this riddle. My remedy was to go down to the clinic to buy medication off the streets from the real junkies on the medication-assisted treatment program. I refused to join the clinic as I knew I could quit on my own. I would go back and forth between MAT and heroin for months.

Finally, my father, who had no idea of my current situation, invited the whole family to go back to London as a reunion of sorts. I picked up 80mg of medication, boarded a night flight to London, and was met by some old friends from my high school days. They served some smoked salmon, cheese, and crackers as a snack. The fish had gone bad, and the next day I got food poisoning and started withdrawals from heroin right in the middle of eating breakfast with my parents. I looked so bad, they suggested I go to their hotel room and lay down for a rest. This was New Year's Eve, the last day of 1984. I ended up taking over their fancy hotel room overlooking Hyde Park, wanting to die. I lay in bed for three days, vomiting with diarrhea. My muscles were rebelling and I had a headache beyond anything I could ever describe.

On the third day, I started to feel a small degree of relief. I remember lying in the shower and muttering a foxhole prayer: "God, please get me through this, and I will never use heroin again." I didn't believe in God, but I was desperate.

After a few weeks, I got back to the U.S. and decided it would be a great idea to go show my junkie friends my newfound sobriety. I ran into an old Puerto Rican buddy named Jay who was excited for me, as he used to sell me dope and would always tell me to take it easy. Jay pulled out a giant glass bong and a small whitish ball that looked like an oily macadamia nut. I vowed to myself that I would never, never touch this stuff he was doing. He dropped the ball into the bong and took a big hit. His eyes rolled back in his head as he exhaled, and I was totally determined that I had no interest. Jay looked at me and asked me if

I wanted a hit.

Without hesitation, I said, of course I would.

Crack, as it would later be called, soon had me by the neck. But no heroin for me – that was my consolation prize. Life got darker than it had ever been before. Six months later, I picked up the heroin again, and now had both crack and dope to contend with.

I knew I needed help. An old friend tried to take me to a 12-Step meeting. He instructed me to just not use before the meeting. I promised him I wouldn't. But I could not keep the promise. My friend told me to come back when I was ready for something different, but he couldn't be around me until then.

Four months later, that same friend called my mother to find out where I was. My mom told him that I was supposed to check into treatment that day. She also told him that they were done with me, and I was no longer part of the family. By this time, I had ripped them off so many times that they had to protect themselves from me.

One day, my friend found me on the streets. He had me tie him off so he could do a shot of dope before taking me to treatment. He eventually got sober again, two weeks after me. He died of

AIDS nine years later, clean and sober.

I went to treatment in 1985 and have not had a drink or a drug since. I did not go there to get sober. I went to treatment for a break from the dark insanity of addiction. I weighed 123 pounds and hadn't bathed in a month. Thirty days later, they sent me to the warm desert of Arizona to check into sober living.

Heroin Anonymous had not been invented yet, so I went to other fellowships. I found my crew there and started on a new journey. I got a sponsor named Fritz, and he started me on this 12-Step path. I didn't believe in God, and he said it didn't matter – he was not concerned. He told me you can take the steps and have a spiritual experience, even as an atheist.

We didn't have cell phones, so making calls to sober members each day was a huge undertaking. Fritz wanted me to reach five sober men per day. Not five dials, but five conversations. I did what he asked me. I carried a tiny spiral notebook in my pocket to write down phone numbers of sober men I could call.

I met a woman in another fellowship who actually paid attention to me. We got married and had a son. The marriage didn't last, as neither of us was very recovered yet. My son is 37 today with two sons of his own. My 92-year-old father, who was convinced his legacy was dead, is now the happiest man on the planet.

My journey continued. I learned about being of service, hospitals and institutions (H&I), and sponsorship. I took a meeting into the jails for 23 years. I finally met my new wife, around seven years into my sobriety. We have been married for 30 years. She is in the rooms as well. We have learned to separate our programs but bring the teachings into our marriage.

At around 29 years sober, I went to a 12-Step convention for freethinkers and agnostics. The keynote speaker was a non-alcoholic, Episcopalian minister. "Hmm," I thought, "Why would this interest me?" But I went anyway, and it changed the trajectory of my sobriety.

The speaker said, "Experience trumps belief." We do not share our *belief*, strength, and hope: we share our *experience*, strength, and hope. I realized that it wasn't that I didn't *believe* in God, I just could not *define* God, and that was enough to keep me stuck. Agnosticism taught me that a definition is not possible, nor is it necessary. That was freeing. I felt a deep sense of relief and no longer judged those of deep faith. I stopped being judgmental and started to find curiosity.

After Fritz died, I got a sponsor named Paul F. After about 10 years of working together, Paul told me he was going to start a new fellowship called Heroin Anonymous and asked if I would be a part of it. When he told me about the singleness of purpose, I disagreed with him and said I would not become a member.

It wasn't until I started sponsoring a guy who was very active in H.A. that I gave it a chance. I was asked to speak at an H.A. meeting. I finally felt the freedom to talk about the insidiousness of heroin addiction. It gave me a lift and a new sense of freedom that is hard to describe.

I learned to love the rooms of Heroin Anonymous, even though many times I am the old man in the room.

Today, I am about to retire from a career of 35 years – all in sobriety. I have two beautiful grandsons. The Twelve Steps not only freed me from the bondage of addiction but also gave me a sense of purpose, character, and integrity. I have become respected in my career, community, and family. I have a loving wife whom I adore and a life worth living. H.A. saved this wretch and turned him into a man!

PIPE DREAMS

Her life was a nightmare, so she stayed numb to cope. Finding H.A. was her step into the sunlight.

I'm one of the few who can't say addiction runs in my family – my father is a pilot and my mom is a nurse. I came from an upper-middle-class family. I had everything I needed or wanted, except for any trace of emotional support or nurturing. My childhood was cold and lonely, and I always had a haunting feeling I was "missing" something. I suffered from anxiety that no other kid around me seemed to be able to relate to, resulting in unbearable migraines. My mom gave me a pain pill for my headaches at 14 years old, and I was never the same again. I hear all the time in the rooms about that first high and feeling as if the world finally fell into place. The sharp edges were finally softened, the unbearable pain subsided, and my racing thoughts were quieted. I was hooked. I couldn't imagine life without that feeling.

At 16, I had an abortion. Along with that, I was prescribed more painkillers. Guilt and shame consumed my soul for that decision, and a day didn't go by that I wasn't high. I lost childhood friends due to the fact that they wanted to drink and smoke weed. However, I wanted to date men who were far too old for me and do molly. I scared them away with my reckless behavior, and I was so alone.

For a while, I was a "functioning" addict – I managed to hold a few jobs, but none longer than maybe a year. I would show up high and dopesick. Several times, I was caught getting high at work. On my first night at college, I overdosed and never went back. I watched my peers move on to finish college, get married, buy houses, and start families, while my shame and guilt continued to pile up so high I couldn't see past the tin foil.

At one of my many jobs, I met a guy. He didn't make me feel shame or guilt for my drug use, because he used like me. He was mentally unwell like me. He was lonely and depressed like me. We fell in love. Unfortunately, we both loved drugs more. I caught him stealing from me and lost it. This was the last straw. I kicked him out, blacking out with rage and saying horrible things.

I slammed the door in his face.

That night, my boyfriend hung himself. The following weeks were a blur. My addiction quickly had me doing things I said I'd never do: having sex for drugs and money, multiple failed suicide attempts, robbing my own family, homelessness, and using the needle, just to name a few. Something I never learned from a young age was any sort of coping skills. The only way I knew how to cope with my grief, shame, and guilt was to throw dope on it. Due to my inability to hold a job, I started selling drugs to support my addiction and pay the rent on the dump of a trap house I was renting.

As a woman living alone in a drug house, I lived in constant fear. I spent years in a stress response, scared of who was at my door, when they would leave, and getting robbed. Several times, I came home to men in my house. I could never let anyone know how afraid I was, though. I wasn't about to give anyone that satisfaction. I thought, "This is a part of the lifestyle."

Looking back, I was almost as addicted to the hustle as I was to the drugs. I finally felt important, needed, wanted – my phone was constantly going off. People seemed to worship me for being their drug dealer, and I was high on how powerful I felt. I knew nothing about naloxone (also known as Narcan) at this point in my addiction, and I can't tell you how many times my friends and I died. It was a daily event. Every day, I was shoving ice down my boyfriend's pants, doing painful sternum rubs, slapping him across the face, and screaming. My nightmare turned into my norm. I didn't see a way out.

I was court-ordered to go to rehab and transported there from my trap house, door-to-door. I was devastated. The judge told me I was looking at eight years in prison, but I couldn't help but think, "At least there's drugs in there."

My house was raided while I was in treatment, and there isn't a doubt in my mind that that was God doing for me what I couldn't do for myself. I fully intended on completing my 30 days, acting as if I was an A+ rehab student, and conning my way back to the only life I knew. God had other plans. I went to sober living in an unfamiliar city with people I did not know. I hated women, and here I was surrounded by them. I was told to go to women's meetings, get a female sponsor, and find sober women to lean on for support. I was horrified. I had always kept the company of men because I could get what I needed from them to support my habit. Women were the competition. Women were the enemy. Women were scary.

One night at a 12-Step meeting, I heard a woman share her story, and I was dumbfounded. She was telling *my* story. I recognized her from other meetings, where she was always smiling and laughing. I hated that. She had this comforting peace about her. I wanted that. She agreed to be my sponsor if I called her and did the work. Something about her made me want to.

Without hesitation, I did everything she suggested to me. She was involved with Heroin Anonymous, so I made it my home group. She was involved in H.A. at the area level, so I got an area-level service position. She helped with H.A. events throughout the year, so I would volunteer to get there early and stay late. My sponsor and Heroin Anonymous were a pivotal part of my recovery journey – they changed everything for me. In Heroin Anonymous, I found people who used like I did, suffered like I had, and were now employable, functioning members of society with homes and social lives. I had no idea such a life could be possible for me. I thought I had gone too far down the scale. I was wrong.

Once I finished the steps with my sponsor, I began taking other women through the steps. I now have a career where I can work with women who are broken and hopeless, just like I once was.

I am in school to become a counselor. I was able to make amends to my loved ones, who all had the same request of me: to stay sober. Each day that I don't pick up is somewhat of a living amends to them. All my friends from the drug house have since passed away. Not one survived this disease or was able to experience this way of life. I like to think I stay sober in their honor.

I'm not sure when exactly I had a spiritual awakening, because I don't think it was a single occurrence. It was like one day I woke up and nothing could make me want to use badly enough to lose the life I had created for myself.

With the help of a Higher Power, my sponsor, Heroin Anonymous, and the women I have met along the way, I have not used a mood- or mind-altering substance in four years. I am grateful for the gift of desperation (GOD) that allowed me to live long enough to see that there is another way. There is hope.

THANK YOU FOR SHARING

I am an addict. My first date of true surrender was in 2018, and this is how I surrender every day: I pray and I meditate. I have a sponsor, and we work the Twelve Steps. I have a sponsee, and we do the same. I go to meetings. I listen to everyone who speaks. I read literature. I stay involved and I volunteer. I am a trusted servant. I give people rides. I call other sober men and women and answer when they call. I practice spiritual principles. I don't have to be right, and I make amends when I am wrong. I remain honest, open-minded, and willing. Gratitude and humility have been my most important lessons. I must practice these vigilantly or else I will give up my best life, this life, for a life not worth living.

But I did not know any of this; someone took their precious time to teach me. Until I humbled myself enough to accept help and guidance, I was just a lonely addict, staggering across this miserable plane to my inevitable end.

So, where did it begin?

If you are reading this story, I imagine things began similarly for both of us. Obviously, we didn't grow up in the same home (unless you're my sister – hi, sis!) or in the same place at the same time. However, if you remember being young and anxious or afraid, always uneasy, never feeling like you fit in quite the way you should, or you felt like you were disguising fear with the mask that is your face, or that people could see the real you right through your eyes, well, then, we felt similarly.

I grew up fortunate. My parents were loving, hard-working, and kind. My mom's discipline was occasionally disproportionate to the "crime," but it was far from abusive. And maybe my dad could have stuck up for me a bit more. But, all things considered, they did their best, and they did a good job. They were raised religious, but our family stopped going to our local church when we were young. Still, even though we weren't raised religiously, my folks demonstrated spiritual principles by being honest, stable, and patient. They made loving sacrifices to ensure we had shoes, electricity, bicycles, doctors, dentists, and a safe home. They didn't consistently have these growing up, so it was important that we did. They helped us with our homework, played with us, made us work, and tucked us in. Still, their sacrifices came with high expectations, so I also grew up with a specter of doubt that haunted me throughout my childhood. Nevertheless, there was no great trauma or tragedy in my upbringing; I grew up wanting for nothing, in a home filled with love.

So, that's why I always did the things. I got the grades; I joined the clubs; I played the part of the good boy. I thought I had to. I thought that others' love for me and acceptance of me were dependent on how I presented myself. In my heart, I don't know why I was like this; no one taught me this. This part of my addiction always existed. I always felt that if they saw me, they wouldn't like me, whoever "they" were. And because I was afraid, I'd spend all my time building the presentation, which resulted in an under-developed concept of self. Regardless, God blessed most of us addicts with cunning, intelligence, and survival instincts. These enabled me to grow up observing others, emulating interactions, and presenting myself successfully.

Let's get back to the story. I wasn't raised around drugs or alcohol. My folks weren't sober, but they weren't teetotalers either. They grew up around alcoholism, and this factored into their choices for their family. It's mind-blowing to have decent genetics, great examples to follow, and yet end up where I did, despite all those advantages. Addiction cares nothing about nature nor nurture. As such, it was a blessing that I didn't find a good opportunity to change the way I felt until roughly the age of 18. That doesn't mean I was oblivious to those who were getting intoxicated, seemingly finding the joy that I was missing. When I observed them, I envied that feeling.

The first time I personally found *it*, I immediately understood. The mix of vodka and orange juice sent a warm, calming rush of relief rolling over me, and I smiled because for the first time, I loved how I felt. Then, a very different rush followed; in the pit of my stomach, I realized that this feeling would be a problem. God granted me that moment of clarity the very first time I drank. I white-knuckled it for a long time thereafter. But that seed of chemical serenity had already taken root, and it would slowly grow until it blossomed into a terrible disease.

Promising my disease that I would tend to it soon, I continued people-pleasing everyone through the next few stressful years of my life. Academically, I'd done well enough in high school to manage a full scholarship to a prestigious university. Despite dabbling mainly with psychedelics and designer drugs, and the occasional brush with authority, I graduated with honors in foreign languages, a full-time job in technology, a dormant addiction, and no clue what was next.

So, what did I do? All the things that I was supposed to do, of course. I doubled down on all the external ambitions that everyone had said would make me happy. I saved some money, got my own place, found a solid career path, pursued marriage, etc. I was a young, eligible bachelor and beginning to throw parties. Those reservations I had about intoxication had finally been swapped for some nice cold beer (or shots). If nothing else, at least drinking temporarily filled the emptiness I still felt inside. I told myself that what I was doing was just innocent fun, but when I looked deep within, I knew I was just buying time.

Eventually, through no fault of her own, I met my future ex-wife at a friend's mixer. We continued bumping into one another, always at a house party, always imbibing. During those get-togethers, I learned that she was a beautiful and talented musician who loved animals, had a stable job, and ambitions for her life. Basically, she checked all the boxes of practicality and compatibility. We had many long conversations, learning that we shared similar values and goals. To this day, I still ask myself if I ever really loved her, or if I loved the idea of her; to this day, I go back and forth. Regardless, while there might have been flourishes of love, that was less important than the fact that on paper we were absolutely perfect for each other. So, we got married. And we drank.

Like all good things built on a lie, the foundation of our relationship began to erode. We were unsatisfied with our jobs. *Glug, glug.* We were unhappy with where we lived. *Smoke, drink.* If we just had things a certain way, it would all be better. *Take a pill.* When none of the coping mechanisms were really working, I fell back on my old ideas. I convinced my wife that we needed to go back to school, get better jobs, and move. Let's keep trying to fix this problem inside of us with something outside. And that's what we did. We distracted ourselves for years in the pursuit of success. Wonderfully for her (and I no longer mean that sarcastically), she achieved fulfillment from her education and her follow-up career as a nurse. I was long jealous of her because she got the satisfaction I was seeking. I just could not understand why the same process was not working for me. I just could not understand my emptiness. Was I not entitled to my own fulfillment?

Looking back at it now, I realize there was a reason I chose nursing. It is respectable and noble. And there were some very fulfilling moments in my early nursing career. As a new grad, my first job was in the burn unit. I promise you this: If you ever want to truly examine every facet of the human condition, try a rotation in The Burn. The job was sweaty, intense, and raw. The rewards were literally lifesaving. Here, for the first time in my life, I could truly empathize, relating my internal pain and emptiness with the physical suffering of my patients. I know the comparison isn't really accurate, for no one suffers like a burn victim, but haven't you ever felt like you were absolutely engulfed in flames, just beneath your skin?

Despite education, experience, accepting work as an ER nurse, and relocating to a new mountain home in the South, which is exactly where I was "supposed to be," the relief of these professional and geographic cures was always short-lived. Emptiness eventually edged out the excitement of the shiny new thing or place. My wife and I did more separately than together, and we realized there wasn't much point to our relationship anymore. Plus, while her alcohol and drug consumption slowed down, I still needed something to fill my emptiness. So, I moved out, and I took my emptiness with me.

As I explored my new mountain town as a "free man," I needed somewhere to go and hide. The hole I found was a local punk rock dive where I became a regular. With nothing and no one else, I would often close the place down with the bartenders, and we would continue to party. On the most fateful of these nights, a bartender invited me over to smoke crack for the first time. Again, I felt a rush of serenity washing over me as that waxy little rock and I melted away together in complete surrender. At the time, I thought that puff of smoke had granted sweet release, but in reality, I had just been blown over the edge. Before crack, I had dabbled in meth and coke, but this is where I first fell to my disease. My first dark surrender.

I would often give my friend a ride to get more crack, treating a nearby apartment complex like a narcotics drive-thru. Countless times, I exchanged hundred-dollar bills and watched a dealer's greasy fingers sprinkle pebbles into my palm. Soon, I was an ER nurse by day and a crackhead by night.

My workplace gave me unbridled access to medical supplies. Because it was a trauma center, our opioid control policies were a little looser than other units. As a nurse, I knew how to find a vein. The transition from crackhead to needle junkie was natural. Inevitable, really. My IV use started with my vanity: I was worried about damaging my teeth from inhaling whatever terrible metallic fumes or chemical impurities my drugs contained. My use further escalated once my ex-wife finally served me with papers. We all have our own darkest times, and this was mine. I used alone at night with a table full of drugs, glass pipes, and needles, knowing that even if I got high, there was still no relief.

Eventually, my escalating use of uppers caused insomnia, repetitive behaviors, and other classic side effects. So, ignoring all my nursing knowledge and experience, rather than seeking help, I decided to supplement my speed with downers. I couldn't pull this off alone, so, like any good junkie, I found my junkie tribe. The disease affects everyone, in every profession, and it somehow allows us to recognize our own. Three of us had discovered how to manipulate the electronic medication system, enabling us to pocket drugs we were supposed to waste. We would reconvene later, combine everything we stole into three syringes, start IVs on one another, and shoot each other up. More than once, I remember blissfully dying and waking up to my coworkers resuscitating me. Amidst those foggy moments, I realized I only found peace when I was literally (not figuratively) high enough to die. But I still believed I had it under control, y'all. When I reflect on that thinking today, I'm dumbfounded that not only could I believe that, but that I absolutely did.

What an awful time to meet the first woman I'd truly love. For once, this wasn't a practical attraction; it was love, indescribable. She made me feel better than I'd ever felt on any substance. I trusted her in a way that I'd never trusted anyone before. She was special; she encouraged me to be my truest self. Using love and acceptance, she saw through my presentation and found the real me.

I swore to myself that I would stop for her, but even love was not enough. Nothing was. For the first time, I was willing to recognize my own powerlessness and unmanageability because I simply could not stop. Compartmentalizing personalities, juggling the lies, and maintaining my image became impossible. I was exhausted.

Remember, I thought I was smarter than everyone else. Throughout my accelerating downward spiral, I believed I was still in total control. I continued to tell myself this, but couldn't believe the lie much longer. A day came when I was full-on sick at work. I was trembling, hot and cold at the same time, nauseous. I'd upgraded from binging to daily IV use. I was doing heroin (or whatever I had) with cocaine on the side and banging more than just the hospital's drugs. Neither of my fellow junkies was working that day, so compelled by the disease and my self-will, I ordered pain medication for a patient who'd already left the floor. The dominoes quickly fell, and soon a coworker was watching me piss away my nursing license with 2 mg of hydromorphone, a heavy-duty narcotic, in my system.

The entire facade that I had carefully built around my life finally burned down, collapsing on me. My RN license was suspended; I was kicked out of my place; my true love left. This was a cleansing by fire, and I was fully exposed for the first time. Strangely, I found relief in those smoldering ashes in the form of acceptance. I didn't know quite how sick my secrets had been making me, but they burned away, too. I was a penniless, unemployed, homeless junkie, and everyone knew it.

It was the first turning point, but I still wasn't quite done.

Let the great white-knuckling begin. The Nursing Board offered a reinstatement program, which I contracted into. The program's restrictions and timeframes were difficult, but I was willing to try it. It was my first real exposure to treatment, but I still thought I knew better than everyone else, and I was still pretending. Meanwhile, my disease waited for any opportunity to relapse. Even though my sobriety was forced and half-assed, my life started getting better. My love returned, wary, but willing. I found a sober roommate through an intensive-outpatient program (IOP). I went to enough recovery meetings to begin applying for health care work again.

One day, I got a urinalysis result back and learned the specific threshold my program used to detect alcohol use. I used my nursing experience and calculated that if I only drank on Fridays, I could get as drunk as I wanted and still pee clean on Monday. So, I hit a bar every Friday, like clockwork. *Only Friday*, my disease swore to me, but every compromise with my disease ends the same. A month-ish later, I was draining my retirement account to buy crack and heroin.

Swiftly thereafter, I finally hit my bottom with a classic overdose. One night, already drunk, my dealer didn't have any speed, so I got a baggie of white and went home. I rigged up, took my shot, and was awakened by the late-morning sun, glaring at me sideways through the dirty glass of a patio door. The cold, concrete floor felt soothing against my broken face, and the golden sunlight painfully glinted off congealing blood. A high-pitched ringing accompanied each heartbeat and a crushing headache. Nauseous, I peeled myself up from the ground. My right eye was black and swollen shut, lids glued into place with blood. Coughing out chunks of aspirated vomit and gasping for air, I stumbled into the living room. My roommate called the paramedics. They arrived shortly and attached me to a monitor, which showed that my vital signs were incompatible with life. The ambulance rushed me to my old ER, where I was profoundly humiliated. The most skilled nurses I'd ever worked with couldn't get a line anywhere on my tracked-up arms. My veins were gone. This humiliating experience was the last thing I remembered before passing into a black, inky emptiness – a feeling you might know all too well.

My coma lasted for six days. As the sedatives wore off, I pieced together memories of my overdose. Loved ones appeared through the haze. I didn't know it, but this would be the last time I ever saw my first true love. I remember crying as wrist restraints prevented me from wiping away the tears. I couldn't even say sorry. Sobbing caused me to choke on the breathing tube down my throat. When the nursing staff extubated me, I cried out with love and pain and begged both my parents and God for help. I will be forever grateful for their unconditional love. This moment of humility was my first true surrender.

I was shipped away, embarrassed yet hopeful, to a 12-Step men's recovery center. Everyone on the campus was in recovery, employees and clients alike. The physicians, leadership, and every counselor – all addicts. They shared relatable stories – stories that demonstrated levels of unmanageability and powerlessness similar to my own. As I listened, I started to recognize that just maybe I didn't know better than everyone else. The more I practiced what I observed, the more meetings I attended, the more my world grew.

The spark of a Higher Power had been ignited within me, and a different flame began to spread. I never knew how close my relationship with the universe could be.

It's been said by others that the work of recovery is simple but not easy. Those counselors, and eventually my sponsors, walked me through the Twelve Steps. I was taught to practice a completely different way of life, or I would die. God-reliance, not self-reliance, was the only way I would ever be fulfilled. I learned to pray and meditate. I began listening more and speaking less. I was shown how to practice the spiritual principles of gratitude and humility. I learned about objective self-inventory. I was taught that I control nothing but my actions.

Over time, I progressed through the Twelve Steps while being reintegrated into my family and society. The promises were already coming true. Spoiler: they still come true every single day, so long as I work the program.

Eventually, the time came to leave the safety of treatment. I'd squandered my meager fortune and my opportunity to have my license reinstated. My parents, kind and giving souls, allowed me to come home with them. I gratefully accepted their help and their rules. Prior to nursing, I had developed some technical skills and good relationships in the tech industry. With my tail between my legs, but an honest heart, an open mind, and a willing spirit, I got an opportunity from a friend that I didn't feel like I deserved. I have since found a new profession, and I am grateful. Today, I demonstrate my gratitude with hard work, reliability, professionalism, and perseverance. I am rewarded with trust, responsibility, financial security, and fellowship.

I was taught, and believed with complete faith, that recovery was my only chance to survive. So, I went to as many meetings as I could. I found a sponsor, and we met weekly and worked the steps. I served my home group and district. At this point in my recovery, Heroin Anonymous was unknown to me, but one day at a local recovery clubhouse, I learned that an H.A. meeting was about to start.

When I walked in, a big country boy with a red afro and beard shook my hand. His eyes smiled genuinely, and he said he was happy I was there. I believed him. A motley crew followed, and their easygoing vibe dispelled my anxiety. They shared their stories, moving me to tears with their honesty, vulnerability, and experience. The depths of their desperation were relatable; their faith and hope gave me goosebumps. H.A. swiftly became my new tribe. As I continue to seek my God and my recovery, my fellows in H.A. show up infinitely more reliably than any dopeman ever did.

In 2019, I became a home group member of a local H.A. meeting. Through trial, tribulation, service, and work, we now represent an area in the South, and our city now has triple the meetings and triple the members. There is an indescribable energy when 80 recovering heroin addicts share a room together, all of us laughing at the same dark jokes and shedding the same tears. Regardless of what we have, we must share it with other addicts, and by doing so, we stop our disease from holding us as lonely hostages. If I've learned anything since getting sober, it's that I actually know very little, and God knows best.

I continue practicing recovery as diligently as I can. It's mainly through H.A., but I've learned it doesn't matter where I seek God, so long as I do. God shows up unfailingly and blesses everyone around me through my recovery. The promises continuously come true in my life, so long as my surrender is continuous.

I have gone through things in my recovery that I couldn't have hoped to navigate without this spiritual program. But I, along with everyone in the program, can only earn serenity with humility and gratitude, and we can only keep it by freely sharing it with others who seek. Thank you for seeking, thank you for sharing, and thanks for letting me share.

A LIFE FULL OF JOY

She faced heartbreak, Hepatitis C, and heroin addiction, but found hope through the H.A. fellowship.

I am a recovering heroin addict living a big, bold, and beautiful life. Without Heroin Anonymous, I would be a dead heroin addict.

I was raised in an upper-middle-class family in the South. I had a mom, dad, sister, dog, swimming pool, and attended a private Christian school. Set up for success, right? But our family dysfunction ate me alive as a child. My mom was often passed out drunk on the couch and would forget to pick me up from school. After my parents' divorce, my friends often weren't allowed to come to my "broken home." I felt like an alien. In my younger years, I learned I was broken and different from everyone else.

My first drug of choice was fantasy: escaping into magical worlds through literature and movies.

I found self-harm in my preteen years. I've always needed something to change the way I feel and cope with negative emotions. I couldn't ever just be.

I remember at the age of 10 or so, my friend asked, "Do you think you'll ever say cuss words?"

I immediately said, "Oh, for sure. And I want to try every drug once."

"Even crack?"

I responded, "Yes – just once, though."

I've been a heroin addict since before I touched drugs. The disease of addiction has lived in my brain as long as I can remember.

Around the age of 14, I made some friends from the public school across the street. These were my people. They had rough family lives like mine and were open about it. I felt connected to this new community. My friends smoked weed and drank, and I was so excited to finally try substances. It wasn't peer pressure; it was a long-time dream of mine. And as I'd expected, I loved using substances. I had arrived. I felt like I needed to use daily. Drugs were the "medicine" that got me on the same level as "normal" people.

Within months of my first time hitting a

joint, I was snorting bath salts in my private school uniform in the school bathroom. You'd think that I would know pretty much immediately that I was an addict. But I needed about six more years of exploring the powerlessness described in Step One until I was convinced.

My sister – my only sibling – passed away suddenly in a car wreck when I was 15. I had just gotten into drugs, and that traumatic loss sent me off to the races. I was high at my sister's funeral and proceeded to put my parents through hell for years, to the point where my dad was preemptively grieving the death of the only child he had left.

My high school years were a mix of wild fun and a chaotic mess. I was known for being the fun party girl, doing drugs in the bathroom and blacking out. I did every drug except for the hardest ones. I was using something every single day, and the days I couldn't find substances were the days I had panic attacks. I was in therapy and on psych meds, but nothing was working or helping.

I'll never forget the moment I first ingested an opiate. It felt like every deeply painful emotion and loss I'd experienced couldn't touch me anymore. A few years later, when I injected an opiate for the first time, it was game over. I didn't even hesitate. After an expulsion from high school for drugs, my friend called me and said he and another buddy had just put an oxy pill in a needle and shot it up. I immediately said, "Come over now and show me."

I'd had dreams of being a psychiatric professional. Having a family. Traveling the world. But the moment I first shot up, my life goals shifted. Now, I just wanted to shoot dope every day.

Months later, after going to college, I made some offbeat friends who, come to find out, were addicts like me. Initially, we clicked because we saw life in the same way. One night, a friend finally opened up to me that he was shooting heroin. I said, "I'm shooting painkillers, so let's get rigs and do it together when the pharmacy opens."

We went to bed, but he never woke up. Days later, after his funeral, I tried heroin for the first time. It was the same dope that had just killed him.

My addiction progressed. I transformed from a social butterfly party girl to a soulless monster. I lost the ability to see beauty in the world. My capacity for love diminished entirely. I could not feel care for myself or others anymore. I have a disease of perception. I justified my use by telling myself, "If you had my life, you'd be a junkie, too." I spent the next few years shooting heroin alone and watching reality TV to at least feel like I had people to use with.

By the age of 20, I had gone from a popular and high-achieving student who was wild, fun, and free, to a dead-inside shell of a human who resembled a gremlin (honestly). My urine turned brown, my stool turned white, and my eyes turned yellow. I had acute Hepatitis C from sharing needles. You'd think I'd be terrified, but I wasn't scared until I woke up from a nod one day and my right hand was paralyzed. I started screaming and crying – not because of potentially losing a limb, but because I am right-handed and I didn't know how to shoot up with my left.

I knew I was dying, but why would I care when there was no other option?

To use is to die. But I believed being sober would end my life from emotional pain. So I kept using.

Then, a former using friend called me from rehab. I recognized her voice, but there was something so different about her. She was honest and vulnerable and happy. I was intrigued. She said the Twelve Steps were changing her life and I should try it. I was willing to do rehab again, if only for the free food and tolerance break. At every 12-Step meeting, I focused on differences. No one mentioned liver failure or robbing people or needles. So what did those people know?

After more treatment centers and psych wards and an arrest, I found myself in a random rehab in another state. I looked like a gargoyle, with wounds on my face and matted hair. My rehab roommate was a dog groomer who was able to pull the mats out of my hair. I was ready to die: I had a two-month prognosis with my liver. But God gave me a sprinkle of willingness, and my ears were open during a hospitals and institutions (H&I) meeting of Heroin Anonymous. In that moment, my life was saved. I couldn't focus on the differences when there were so few. These people spoke my language, my story, and then they spoke about this crazy thing called recovery. They swore they didn't want to use anymore, nor did they want to die. What was this magic? I ran up to them after, and they told me about sponsorship and the Twelve Steps. I figured I'd try it for a year and if it sucked, I'd go back out.

I'll be honest: my willingness to try the program was influenced by falling in love in early recovery with a man in Heroin Anonymous who was restarting his recovery. I wanted to be with him, and he was doing the Twelve Steps and sober living. So I decided to do it, too.

Pretty soon, I started working the program for myself. I put the effort I used to put into chasing dope into working the steps. My first H.A. meeting outside of rehab was similar to my first heroin high. I felt seen. I felt hope. My sponsor was hardcore. Think scary, militant vibes. She suggested I call her every day, get an H.A. home group, accept a service position, get women's numbers in H.A., clean up, help with coffee, and fellowship by spending time with other sober women. I did all these things. We worked the steps thoroughly in just six months. I started sponsoring the day I finished Step 12. My obsession to use was lifted. My first few months, I spent eight hours a night dreaming of trying to get dope. My brain was fighting abstinence and the solution so hard, but the Twelve Steps won in the end.

While I am an alcoholic and an addict of many substances, Heroin Anonymous has always been my home. I like to say it's an edgier version of other 12-Step fellowships. The level of authenticity and relatability is unprecedented.

Fifteen months into my recovery, the man I'd fallen deeply in love with relapsed. And that relapse left him dead on the floor of my bedroom. I knew I couldn't survive this. But that day, I had done my prayer and meditation and I had been of service to other heroin addicts. It was like I had armor on. I begged my grand-sponsor to let me knock myself out with gas station cold medicine and not count it as a relapse. On my way to see my partner's body before it went into a body bag, I stared at the pavement as the car traveled at 80 miles per hour down the highway. I considered jumping out. But my recovery program shielded me from this, just for that day.

The next day, I moved in with my sponsor, who was eight months pregnant, with a toddler and a husband in a 900-square-foot home. Those next few months, I worked the program despite wanting to die. And I grieved sober. Years later, I am still sober. My sponsor named her newborn son after my partner who died. The bonds made in this program are otherworldly.

I have been on fire for this program for close to a decade now. Some are sicker than others, and when I'm complacent, my perspective on life gets sick very fast. *Woe is me. I'm the victim. This isn't fair.* When I'm locked into that perspective, heroin seems like a great idea. The best idea. As a loved one in my H.A. home group says, "Rent is due every day." I have to maintain my recovery program every day in order to benefit from this complete change of perception I've experienced.

When I got sober, I began to have dreams for my life again. I am so glad, looking back, that God had other plans for me. I moved across the country to a beautiful new home in the mountains. I crowdsurf, dance in the moshpit, go to sunrise sets at music festivals, and travel internationally – sober. I've learned to love again. And none of this would be possible or even enjoyable if I wasn't still hitting meetings, serving my home group, talking to sponsees daily, writing nightly inventories, re-working the steps, and laughing until my stomach hurts from dark jokes during a post-H.A. meeting fellowship. Most days, the maintenance steps are as natural as brushing my teeth and drinking water.

My hand regained function after some months – it was a pinched nerve. My liver healed and my Hep C was cured. I became a counselor. On the other hand, my mom never got sober, and most of my friends from high school overdosed and died, including the friend I shot up with for the first time. Why him and not me? I've determined it's not my business. That's God's business.

So, what will I do with this life I still have? I was asked to give eulogies at my old friends' services. My dad went from considering me dead to calling me for advice. Strangers ask me what my secret is – why I'm so joyous. I joke that I was blessed with this cute thing called heroin addiction, which led me to a design for living that really works. My life is full of purpose. I contribute to the stream of life. I love myself. And I know I will lose everything in the blink of an eye if I forget why I am where I am today. Heroin Anonymous saved my life, and I'm going to make the best of it.

GIVEN THE GIFT OF DESPERATION

She was born with a rare illness and chronic pain that normalized her opioid use. Learning to be honest with herself was the key to finding relief.

When I was born, I was diagnosed with a rare illness that would land me in and out of hospitals most of my life. I was in constant pain and never learned to be a kid. I remember I was in a stroller for a long time instead of a wheelchair, because we couldn't afford one. I was made fun of, bullied, and alienated. My own sister wanted nothing to do with me because of the bullying and the embarrassment.

I was prescribed codeine and oxycodone for pain starting at the age of five. I couldn't walk or even go to school for a while. I would be stuck in bed, alone with my books and medication. Loneliness became my norm, as my dad would be gone most of the day and come home late at night, my sister was always at a friend's house, and my mom was a flight attendant, gone for a week at a time. Once, when I was home alone, my mom left the liquid codeine bottle with a note on the kitchen counter. I remember getting home from school, taking the codeine bottle off the counter, sitting on the kitchen floor, and drinking about half the bottle. I was nine.

Growing up in and out of hospitals, I had a group of friends who had other rare illnesses. Most of them didn't live long enough to reach their 18th birthday, 10th birthday, or even a year. I attended a lot of funerals when I was very young. Everyone always seemed so okay with the fact that a child had just died, and when I asked my mom why, she said, "Because they are not in pain anymore." I couldn't grasp the concept of death, but not being in pain anymore? That's what I wanted.

I had many suicide attempts in my life, just wanting the pain to end. I was adopted young and never had a real connection with anyone. I had a serious fear of questions and authority. I always lied about what I was doing, even if I didn't need to. I was alone a lot in middle school, and I learned how to "cope" with being alone by using or going on adventures deep into the city by myself.

Around high school, my health started to get better, but I was still prescribed opioids and benzodiazepines. Starting public school for the first time, I found out my medication was worth a decent amount of money. I started dealing my meds and finding other drugs. Then, I wasn't alone in the house as much because I found people who used drugs like me. I was 15, hanging out with people in their late twenties. One of their moms had a prescription for oxy, and I started smoking it daily. It got to the point where I wasn't able to hide my addiction anymore. I got in trouble in school, was suspended, and was ordered to go to 12-Step meetings in order to finish my tech program. I went to meetings but never listened. If anything, I was listening for ways to sneak around and still get away with my use.

I barely graduated from high school: Truthfully, I think they just wanted me out of there. I moved in with my boyfriend at the time. We met at a meeting. I thought we would get clean together, but within three or four months, I tried heroin for the first time. I remember the wave going through my body, and the warmth I felt. All my life, I felt alone, but for the first time, I felt truly connected to myself, a drug, and another person. This is all I wanted in my life at the time.

I don't know when the physical abuse started. I lost count of the beatings and humiliation. I lost count of the times I cried, ran away, and came back. I lost count of the hospitalizations and all of the questions. I lost count of the friends I lost because I chose my boyfriend and heroin.

We were dealing drugs together. We did everything together. I was always supervised. People were tired of seeing me abused and wanted to help me get out. Our dealer began to sneak me my own supply to sell so I could make money to leave the state. He opened a door for me, taking a financial hit to help an 18-year-old girl escape the grips of complete devastation.

I began to sell heroin in the dorms of a prestigious college in the middle of the night while my boyfriend slept. One night, he was awake and waiting for me when I came home. He thought I was cheating. I didn't know what to say, so instead I gave him the money I made that night, hoping that would be the end of it. He screamed at me for hours, breaking me down more and more by the minute. For me, it wasn't worth sneaking around. I decided to start using the supply I was given to soften the blows, emotionally and physically.

Eventually, I did leave. I fled to my grandmother's house; she was in hospice. I was out in the city alone, looking for heroin on my own. I always had my boyfriend, and I guess never truly realized that he kept me safe from others on the street, who stayed away out of fear. Once, I got in the car with someone I barely knew. He drove past our destination. My heart went into my stomach at each exit we passed. I kept asking him where we were going, and all he would say was, "I am sorry, I am so sorry."

I tried to jump out of the car on the freeway, was hit in the head, and just froze. I don't remember much. He was trying to transport me out-of-state to go God-knows-where. I tried escaping and failed, which had horrific repercussions. The second time I tried to escape, I succeeded. I didn't know where I was because I was so disoriented from the drugs. All I could hear was the overwhelming sound of the freeway. I ended up down by the river, trying to clean my body of the rotten feeling of all the touches I had endured. I lay there sobbing, praying that God would protect my family as I felt a little splash of water wash over my fingertips. If it wasn't for a group of kids who found me, I would've died. They called the police. I had been missing for three days.

I left my home state for treatment. It was

during the COVID-19 pandemic, so I didn't build much of a community except for the women I went to treatment with. I graduated from that program and went back into tech work. Things were going well, until they weren't. I was subpoenaed in an attempted murder case. I couldn't get out of it. I pleaded a mental health defense: seeing my ex and going down that road wasn't good for my recovery. However, my plea was denied due to the severity of this case. I felt that I couldn't escape my past, no matter how hard I tried.

I began to use fentanyl again after being dry from substances for a year. I began to cross lines in my addiction I had never crossed before. It landed me with a warrant for my arrest, and I spent a night in jail before I decided to get myself into treatment again so I could avoid further charges. I returned to the same treatment center, thinking I could manipulate the system. I broke all of the rules – I lied to everyone. I wouldn't let anyone in. I just wanted them to sign a paper so I could avoid jail time.

On Christmas Day, I left the program and relapsed and overdosed. I was given the gift of desperation, realizing I didn't want to live like this anymore. I called my sponsor and the treatment center, and they let me back in. The treatment center gave me a second chance. People from H.A. offered me hugs and welcomed me back in with open arms. It gave me hope that I could do this. I got very honest, and I opened up about things I promised myself I'd take to the grave.

I have tried so many different types of meetings, but for me, Heroin Anonymous has become my home. My home group members have been there through thick and thin, through panic attacks and sleepless nights. They've helped me with jobs and fun adventures. I have built a community and feel as if I am not alone. I have hope for a future, a future where I can build roots and no longer have to run away. My past may come back up again, but it doesn't lead me back to dope because I'm working a program.

My sponsor asked me for three things when I started this program: honesty, open-mindedness, and willingness. From those three things, I have gained so much more than I could've ever imagined. I am able to manage chronic pain without drugs or alcohol. I am able to cry and feel feelings after being numbed out my whole life. I am able to be who I want to be instead of who I thought people wanted me to be. I am following my dreams, which I never thought were obtainable. I'm exploring my passion for art in all forms. I feel safe, seen, and connected.

All the things I thought I could get through drugs, I have found tenfold in the rooms of Heroin Anonymous.

ESCAPING MY DOUBLE LIFE

*Her heroin addiction led to losing her children
and ending up in the court system. Sobriety
was her pathway to a better life.*

I am a heroin addict. I last used in 2021. I grew up in a normal, loving household. The problem was me and the way I felt about myself. I was uncomfortable in my own skin. Since I was always more comfortable with animals than people, I went to school to be a veterinary technician during high school. That's when I discovered weed and alcohol. They quieted the noise in my head on the weekends when I would binge drink. I've never done anything in normal amounts. I made it through high school, and we had a graduation party. We had gotten ecstasy for the party. That led to two years of raving on the weekends and doing cocaine. I was "fully functional" at this time. I had a job and my drug use didn't get in the way of my life – yet.

When I was 20, I met the father of my kids. We ended up being together for 17 years. I started using heroin with him almost immediately. I was still working, able to function while living the double life we all live. I became pregnant when I was 20, and I was in full-blown heroin addiction at the time. I don't know how the doctors didn't know, or anyone.

I continued to use heroin and opioids, off and on, for years. At one of the low points of my addiction, I was writing false prescriptions for oxycodone for my cats. I was finally caught and arrested. I ended up getting a disorderly persons ticket. That time, my whole family learned what was going on. I went to a 12-Step meeting with my aunt, and I remember sitting in a circle with a group of old women, thinking, "Oh, I don't have a problem like them. I just like to do drugs."

Fast forward to 2013. My kids' father and I were stuck deep in a nine-month run. We had three kids by then. He admitted to his family what was going on, and they ended up calling Child Protective Services on us. The social worker came in and removed our kids. My partner and I began the process of getting them back.

We cleaned up our lives, painting a pretty picture on the outside. On the inside, we were definitely still broken. We stayed broken until our next huge relapse in 2018. My partner was doing fentanyl, and I had picked up a bad crystal meth habit. Child Protective Services became involved again when I was arrested. We were dodging the social worker while my mother was living with us because we needed supervisors to be around our children. Then, right before Christmas, my husband and I were arrested on serious felony charges. The kids were removed again, my family stopped talking to us, and away we went on an even harder run with more and more criminal activity.

In May 2018, I was told I had mandatory drug court. I ended up leaving, and a no-bail warrant was issued for me. I was caught a week later. At 37 years old, I ended up going to jail for the first time in my life. When they talk about how progressive this disease is, they're telling the truth. I would have never thought I'd end up where I was.

I would continue in the drug court system for three-and-a-half years. I ended up graduating. About two months before I graduated, I lost two of my best friends to overdoses, only a week apart. I was managing the sober living home I was living in, and I decided to make the change in my life – to finally get a sponsor and give this whole program a try.

I was 18 months sober when I found my sponsor. She took my hand and put it into the hand of God. At two years sober, I went through Steps Five, Six, and Seven. I started making amends. My life got better. My daughters wanted to have a relationship with me.

Today, I sponsor women and speak at multiple rehabs as a member of H.A. I have an H.A. home group and have found my tribe of addicts – people who used like I did. Who else can I talk to about sticking needles in my arm and not get judged? Today, I can use my story to help the next suffering heroin addict.

H.A. saved my life and gave me back the life I deserve today. Today, I'm employable and trusted with a key to my job. I can help even more women find the program and the way to a better life. God saved me, so I can do His work and help the next suffering addict.

SAFE INSIDE MYSELF

She relapsed for thirty years and couldn't stay sober on her own. H.A. gave her the longest period of sobriety since childhood.

When I was born, the joke was that I was the prettiest baby in the NICU. My mom had gained less than 20 pounds during her pregnancy, and she and I both almost died when her blood pressure dropped during my birth. My dad disclosed their drug use in case it might save us, and maybe it did. When my levels stabilized, I was sent home with my grandparents.

My parents' marriage was by all accounts a four-year nightmare, mostly driven by my father's addiction and charisma. When it ended, Dad immediately returned to his life as an alcoholic drifter, in and out of jail, relationships, treatment facilities, and the rooms of 12-Step fellowships. He was often locked up for theft, drugs, and vagrancy. His disease took him at 47.

Mom decided to take a shared ride notice off a bulletin board and travel. I stayed with my grandparents, as I wasn't invited. When she returned a year later, I did not know her.

My childhood was confusing and painful. When I stayed with Mom, we moved often, and she seemed to work constantly. I was left alone in basement apartments a lot. Mostly, I lived with my grandparents and three uncles.

My grandparents lived in a beautiful Victorian. I loved my grandmother desperately, but it was not a happy home. My grandfather could be cruel to us and it did not always feel safe. I was terribly lonely, and I felt like I did not belong and was not wanted. I was often left unattended. My first suicide attempt was at 12. I do not know who in my family bandaged my wrist or how close I came to succeeding. There were no doctors. My mom's family did not and still do not believe in outside intervention. At some point, Child Protective Services became involved, due to serious allegations of neglect and sexual abuse, and I stayed with a foster mother for about a year.

I was having difficulty in school academically and socially, and my grandparents became concerned about my education, so they put me in a private school. I went from always being new to the neighborhood, to being a terrified imposter surrounded by wealthy kids, most of whom had traditional families.

It was hard to pretend I was just like the other kids when I never knew where I would wake up. If I was with my mom, I might show up at school in a beater car, hungry and improperly dressed. If I was with my grandparents and extended family, other types of abuse might have occurred. I learned, or was taught, to be careful about what I said about my home life and that my appearance could influence people's perception of me. I was a pretty kid.

My mom often reminded me that I was my father's daughter, that I had an addictive personality and could end up just like him if I took even one drink. But I saw people in her family using successfully and being somewhat productive members of society. I was smarter than most of them, and I figured I had a 50/50 shot at being normal. So, I ignored her advice. Whenever possible, I spent time with public school kids – first on the playground, then in suburban basements, and then in clubs and music venues. Drugs and alcohol were a way of life.

My private school friends were not much different from the kids in my neighborhood. We never went to the mall without vodka to spike our diet sodas or something acquired from an older sibling or parent's medicine cabinet. Although generally passive, I was a leader when it came to finding ways to get loaded. I often had older boyfriends willing to get us drunk or high. Weekends were generally a blur from junior high on.

My "partying" progressed as I aged and accelerated when I moved in with my mom as a young teenager and had much less supervision. When I first tried an opiate, I felt like I had found a home for the first time. I was safe inside myself. My core was protected from the pain and chaos of the world and the people in it. I wanted to feel that way all the time.

The first time I was dopesick, I vowed to stop. I did not. Instead, my addiction became a part of my identity. I immersed myself in a drug and music culture where I felt I could be myself. But even among "cool" people, my drug use was seen as extreme. I moved away from anyone who tried to get between me and using. Heroin would go on to be the love of my life, my closest friend, and my protector.

When I went to college, I took my addiction along. I eventually graduated with a C average. Not everyone fared as well. Many people I turned on to drugs were arrested, became homeless, or died. My college roommate dropped out and was murdered while living and working on the streets. Escaping these consequences reinforced my idea that I could manage my addiction and didn't need help. I did make a loose connection between my addiction and my suffering. I attempted suicide through overdose several times, never admitting to others that had been my intention.

I tried to stop using heroin many times through various means such as therapy, medication-assisted treatment (MAT), relationships, and moving. I refused to consider treatment or a 12-Step program. The 12 Steps were for people who could not handle their own lives – people like my father. I could handle myself. To me, that meant I could detox myself cold turkey or buy meds on the street. I could work to pay my rent or get someone to pay it for me or take me in. I could get little bits of time off heroin, but I would still be drinking and using other drugs. During these "clean" times, I would often be able to rebuild my life. But I would soon pick up again and tear everything down.

For an intravenous drug user, I did a good job of hiding my addiction, or at least better than many. Sometimes, I was very high functioning, and I successfully used skills developed in childhood to help me get over. I lived a double life and could switch between the drug world and the straight world. I took care with my appearance and was very secretive, so I was often able to maintain legitimate jobs for a time, although sometimes I did things to feed my addiction that were dangerous or that I knew were immoral.

I wanted a change, so I moved to another state. I soon gave up trying to stay abstinent and for a couple dark years leaned into a lifestyle I would once have found unimaginable. When a boyfriend tried to kill me, my family dragged me back home. I was too weak to fight them – probably because I was experiencing liver failure. Back home I started relying heavily on MAT for any time at all off heroin. I could live an almost-normal life for a while before invariably cycling back to heroin and despair. My estimate is that I never had more than three months sober in any given year before joining Heroin Anonymous.

During one of these almost-normal times, I got married. I really wanted love and to have a family. My husband was a newly sober alcoholic, and we moved to his home in England. We thought that love and music would keep us from using. It did not.

We moved back to my home state, and I got a good job. But I was still relapsing several times a year. I could never stay stopped and almost lost my hand to cellulitis while running a successful social service program. It seemed as soon as I got myself under control, my husband lost his struggle with alcohol and other drugs. We stayed together for a decade before a painful and lengthy breakup.

The relapse that led me to detox was rough. My addiction had progressed, and the drugs had also changed. Although fentanyl had been creeping into the heroin supply for years, now it was the only game in town. I don't know how long my run was, but at the end, I was using 3 grams of fentanyl a day. I was also using against my will in a way I had never before. I was totally isolated and most of my time was spent picking up when I was supposed to be working or using alone in my room. I was getting close to being exposed at work and my appearance was suffering. But this time I did not really care.

By the end, I was propping myself up at night with pillows to breathe. I was asking a man no longer speaking to me to watch my late-night shot and walk me around the block when I could not easily lift my chest to breathe. I tried to kick on my own like I had many times before. It was too physically painful. My ex was watching me die; repeatedly dragging me back from the edge was horrible for both of us. He begged me to go to detox, and I agreed because I felt like I was drowning. Now, I know that feeling was respiratory depression.

I was terrified of being locked up. If my breathing and thinking had been normal, I would not have consented to detox. I would have died while figuring out a way to stop on my own.

One of the reasons I agreed to be admitted to a public hospital was that I heard I could use in the waiting room bathroom while they ran my insurance. In my mind, I was going to avoid the worst of the withdrawals then get the hell out of there. In reality, they cannot legally give you enough medication to make you well when you have been using like I was at the end. I was in full-blown withdrawal in a shared room with three other women and nurses that took my blood pressure every time I fell asleep. I could not eat at all. I could barely keep down water or liquid medication. Only my estranged husband knew exactly where I was. My despair and loneliness were as deep as they were in my childhood.

I was so sick that it was hard to figure out how to leave. At detox, one woman in my room was nice to me. So, when she asked me to go to a meeting with her to keep a creepy man from sitting next to her, I went. The group doing outreach to hospitals and institutions (H&I) were late, so we sat around telling war stories with the male patients. We started talking about first times, and I realized that if I survived until my birthday, I would have been using heroin for exactly 30 years. I thought, "30 years, how pathetic is that?"

I realized it was hopeless, and I would never be free of this. That I had nothing to live for. I decided that I would wait until the meeting was over, get my 8 p.m. meds, and use that strength to demand my clothes and leave. I had been paid while I was in there; I was never paying rent again. Every time I had tried to kill myself with dope before, I had failed. It's hard to afford enough heroin to intentionally OD when you reach that stage of desperation. But I knew fentanyl would kill me.

Silently, my most horrific memories and experiences so painful I had mostly blocked them out started to flash before my eyes in quick succession. It was like the death scene in an old movie. My life as a junkie flashed before my eyes.

I came back into awareness of my body and the world outside of my head and realized there was a meeting going on around me. The first thing I heard the speaker say was that he had been relapsing on heroin for 40 years. I thought simply, "That's longer than 30."

This man said he had found a way to stop using heroin and a better way of life. A life with some happiness that was worth living. I had never had happiness like he described; I had never had serenity or anything close to it, outside of a needle. I believed he was telling the truth. I thanked the speaker and left the meeting with a tiny bit of hope.

I made a decision to give recovery a try. After all, I had literally nothing to lose. I stayed in detox and agreed to do everything that my counselor had been suggesting. I agreed to an intensive outpatient program (IOP), weekly urine tests, and attending 90 meetings in 90 days – all while working full time and living with my ex. Recovery was scary, exhausting, and painful, both physically and emotionally. I was about to give up when someone brought me to a Heroin Anonymous meeting.

Today, I am continuously sober for the longest time since childhood. Although I believe grace brought me into the fellowship of Heroin Anonymous, I work a vigorous program to stay here. I go to meetings, have a home group, work the Twelve Steps, and I'm in service to others. I found the identification that kept me in the rooms and the fellowship that helped me slowly become part of the world again.

A PATH TO FREEDOM

This sober inmate is dedicated to carrying the message to his fellows in state prison. The spiritual solution works, no matter where we are.

I'm currently writing this as an inmate in a state prison in the Midwest. For more than two decades, I've been in and out of prison. But even though I am incarcerated, my message is one of gratitude and hope. Because of God, the Twelve Steps, and the fellowship of Heroin Anonymous, I have a blueprint for success. I have a path to freedom, and I know how to find it and walk it.

I was born and raised in the Bay Area in California. My childhood was short-lived, but I still have some great memories: riding BMX all over town, taking the train to the city, skateboarding, rope swinging at the creek, listening to music, and partying with the older crowd. Life was an adventure.

I was the oldest of three kids in a single-parent home. I saw drugs, alcohol, and violence daily. My grandmother was a pot dealer, as were my aunts and cousins. They built custom lowriders. All their friends were gangsters, dealers, and addicts. My mom drank and used, too. Mom said I was the "man of the house," and I think I took that quite literally. As a result, my childhood didn't last long.

Smoking cigarettes and drinking alcohol came naturally. I started smoking weed at 11 and snorted my first line at 13. I was using amphetamines like a pro by the time I was a teenager.

When my mom moved us to a different part of the state, I hated her for it. I made up my mind that I would be as defiant as I possibly could. I did whatever I wanted when I wanted. Drugs made all my pain and anger go away, but it was always temporary, so I turned it way up. Soon, I was out of control.

I lived without respect for anyone. I broke my mom's things. I was high all the time. I started hanging around older Mexican guys connected to the cartel and started making money by selling drugs. I was all for it. By the time I was 15 years old, I was selling speed and coke. At 17, I dropped out of school. I sold drugs and had a full-time job at a big box store. I had no idea how bad my addiction was.

I didn't realize how sick I was until my main connection got locked up. Suddenly, I no longer had an unlimited supply to match my monster habit. Life got really, really hard. Addiction turned me into someone I said I would never be. I would never be a felon. I would never use needles. I would never use heroin. Yet, I did all these things and more. By 20, I was in jail.

I know this sounds like a nightmare. To be honest, it has been. However, I have to tell you about a miracle I experienced when I was 25 years old, sitting in jail and feeling defeated. At that time, I was given the gift of desperation. I had no idea how to change, but I knew I needed help. My oldest cousin told me he had gotten clean. His addiction was as bad as mine: he was the worst of the worst. But somehow, he'd changed. He looked different, sounded different. In recovery, he was someone I'd never met before.

All I knew was if he could do it, then I could do it. He told me about the Twelve Steps and the treatment program he graduated from. He told me about the sober living home where he lived. As he shared his story, he helped me follow a sober path. I found a sponsor and my way into the steps.

Obviously, my story doesn't end here. Thirteen years after my miracle in jail, I moved closer to my mom and brother. They'd relocated years prior to the Midwest, and I was desperate for a new start. That December, I found a fresh start – in the county jail. I caught a case and was on my way to prison once again.

During that stay in prison, I was introduced to Heroin Anonymous by a man in recovery who spoke to us inmates. His experience, strength, and hope landed on fresh ears. He told us how drugs were never his problem. Sobriety was his problem. He could handle using, but couldn't stand to draw a sober breath. That made a lot of sense to me. After the meeting, I talked to him and told him what I had been through. I sheepishly told him that I needed help – again. I asked if he knew anyone who would visit me, and this stranger's immediate response was, "I'll visit you, man."

That man became my sponsor and has since been my recovery mentor and good friend. When I was released, he picked me up from prison and brought me to sober living. I found a home group, worked the Twelve Steps, and sponsored others. I learned how to maintain my spiritual condition with prayer and meditation.

I also got involved in service at the group level. First, I was a General Service Representative (GSR) chairing a meeting. I served as the Area's Chair of Hospitals and Institutions (H&I). While in this position, I started two new meetings to support people in treatment facilities. It's hard to describe the value and purpose this gave me. When you've gotten clean many times, you start to wonder if there is a secret to staying clean. Through helping others, I finally found an identity worth having.

I relapsed many, many times, but I also learned the truth about myself – a truth that has guided me to look at my recovery again and again. I stubbornly kept trying to find the right combination, order, and amount of drugs, alcohol, people, sex, and material things. I used the same unsuccessful tactic with recovery, trying to pick and choose. Everything I tried my way didn't work. As an addict and convict, I still had to face the void between my old life and the new one I could have.

I never thought the hell I've lived through could help others, but it's now a passion. I was even available to my brother when he was at his worst and needed help with addiction. Thankfully, he found recovery, and he's been clean and sober ever since. We had a toxic past relationship, but now we're close, and he is truly an inspiration to me.

I'd love to tell you that this is where I floated off into the sunset on a pink cloud, singing a song and farting rainbows. That's not what happened. I let up on my spiritual program of action. I stopped praying, stopped meditating. The spiritual principles I learned to live by dissolved. Solitude turned into loneliness. Using became a solution. In this short period of time, I overdosed twice. I lost everything I owned, even my freedom.

However, no matter how low my addiction has taken me, Heroin Anonymous is still here for me. During this incarceration, I've done the Twelve Steps to the best of my ability. I've been able to guide a few of my fellow inmates through the steps as well. My release is coming soon. I'm excited to retrace my previous path to freedom, with meetings, sponsorship, service, and unity. H.A. showed me how to be a son, brother, sponsor, friend, and a man. No matter what, I have purpose today. I hope to see you soon.

Appendix

In this section, you'll find the resources you need to run a meeting of Heroin Anonymous.

Additional readings and formats can be found at www.heroinanonymous.org. We have found these resources helpful, as they allow us to focus on carrying the message in a language that is honest and clear.

None of these resources is exhaustive. We believe that as our fellowship continues to reach new members, we will continue to evolve. Fresh ideas, inspiration, and insights are vital to keeping Heroin Anonymous alive and healthy – and ready to help the next suffering addict.

A WAY OUT

*This reading is often used at the beginning of
H.A. meetings and includes our 12 Steps.*

Many of our members have gotten sober lots of times. Our challenge was staying sober. We were able to stop using for days, months or even years, but we could not find a permanent solution. Eventually, we wound up in rooms like these. If you are a heroin addict desperately searching for a way out, we found one that's working for us.

We all had our own ideas on how to stop using. These methods didn't work for long. If these approaches were successful, we would have quit a long time ago. Holding on to these beliefs was futile and until we were able to let go altogether, we could never be free. We discovered a better way to live. We saw others who no longer struggled with heroin addiction and even seemed happy! They encouraged us to go through the

Twelve Steps like they had.

By applying these principles in our daily lives, we found a new freedom, a new happiness and a new way of living. We have found that successful recovery is dependent upon completion of all Twelve Steps. If you want a way out and are willing to work for it, then you are ready to begin. Here are the steps we took:

1. We admitted we were powerless over heroin and all other opioids – that our lives had become unmanageable.[1]

2. Came to believe that a Power greater than ourselves could restore us to sanity.

3. Made a decision to turn our will and our lives over to the care of God, as we understood Him.

4. Made a searching and fearless moral inventory of ourselves.

5. Admitted to God, to ourselves, and to another human being the exact nature of our wrongs.

6. Were entirely ready to have God remove all these defects of character.

---

1. Step 1 was edited to reflect changes made at the 2025 World Service Conference.

7. Humbly asked Him to remove our shortcomings.

8. Made a list of all persons we had harmed, and became willing to make amends to them all.

9. Made direct amends to such people wherever possible, except when to do so would injure them or others.

10. Continued to take personal inventory and when we were wrong promptly admitted it.

11. Sought through prayer and meditation to improve our conscious contact with God as we understood Him, praying only for knowledge of His will for us and the power to carry that out.

12. Having had a spiritual awakening as the result of these steps, we tried to carry this message to heroin addicts, and to practice these principles in all our affairs.

When we sincerely applied the 12 Steps to our lives, we found long term success in sobriety. We are not asked to do this perfectly; we strive for spiritual progress rather than spiritual perfection.

We have found a way out of our suffering and simply wish to share what worked for us. In our fellowship you will see heroin addicts helping each other, freely passing on their experience to those who are desperately searching for an answer to their own heroin addiction.

PREAMBLE

This reading is often used at the beginning of meetings to share what H.A. is and is not.

Heroin Anonymous is a fellowship of people who share their experience, strength, and hope with each other that they may solve their common problem and help others to recover from heroin and opioid addiction. The only requirement for membership is a desire to stop suffering from heroin and opioid addiction. There are no dues or fees for H.A. membership; we are self-supporting through our own contributions. H.A. is not allied with any sect, denomination, politics, organization or institution; does not engage in any controversy, neither endorses nor opposes any causes. Our primary purpose is to stay sober and help other heroin or opioid addicts to achieve sobriety.

NO MORE SUFFERING

This reading is often used at the end of H.A. meetings.

There are those of us who no longer suffer from heroin addiction; it is our hope to share the solution that we have found. The Twelve Steps have rocketed us into a new dimension of freedom. The God of our understanding has commenced doing for us what we could not do for ourselves. We have been restored to sanity and have been liberated from the bondage of self. As we work the simple program of action the promises materialize in our lives. We hope our message will encourage those who still suffer to work this program honestly and thoroughly. The connection to our Higher Power guides our lives, empowers the step work process, and unites our fellowship. Our past has uniquely qualified us to help those that still suffer from heroin addiction. We have been equipped with the Power to carry this message to those who have a desire for a new way of life. It is our hope that any heroin addict who seeks this message shall find it freely in the fellowship of Heroin Anonymous.

SINGLENESS OF PURPOSE

This reading is often used at the beginning of meetings to describe who H.A. is for.

H.A. is a group of heroin addicts helping other heroin addicts achieve sobriety through the Twelve Steps. In keeping the focus on heroin addiction in our meetings, we are providing a place where addicts can come together and share about their common problem, addiction to heroin, as well as the common solution. In maintaining our singleness of purpose, we recognize our limitations, but we ensure that the heroin addict will always have a place they can go to find recovery. Heroin Anonymous wishes to include all people who suffer from opiate and opioid addictions into the classification of "heroin addict," as we believe there is little difference in getting free from these substances.

THE TWELVE
STEPS OF HEROIN
ANONYMOUS

1. We admitted we were powerless over heroin and all other opioids – that our lives had become unmanageable.

2. Came to believe that a Power greater than ourselves could restore us to sanity.

3. Made a decision to turn our will and our lives over to the care of God, as we understood Him.

4. Made a searching and fearless moral inventory of ourselves.

5. Admitted to God, to ourselves, and to another human being the exact nature of our wrongs.

6. Were entirely ready to have God remove all these defects of character.

7.   Humbly asked Him to remove our shortcomings.

8.   Made a list of all persons we had harmed, and became willing to make amends to them all.

9.   Made direct amends to such people wherever possible, except when to do so would injure them or others.

10. Continued to take personal inventory and when we were wrong promptly admitted it.

11. Sought through prayer and meditation to improve our conscious contact with God as we understood Him, praying only for knowledge of His will for us and the power to carry that out.

12. Having had a spiritual awakening as the result of these steps, we tried to carry this message to heroin addicts, and to practice these principles in all our affairs.

THE TWELVE TRADITIONS OF HEROIN ANONYMOUS

1. Our common welfare should come first; personal recovery depends upon H.A. unity.

2. For our group purpose there is but one ultimate authority – a loving God as He may express Himself in our group conscience. Our leaders are but trusted servants; they do not govern.

3. The only requirement for H.A. membership is a desire to stop suffering from addiction to heroin and all other opioids.

4. Each group should be autonomous except in matters affecting other groups or H.A. as a whole.

5. Each group has but one primary purpose–to carry its message to the heroin

and/or opioid addict who still suffers.

6. An H.A. group ought never endorse, finance, or lend the H.A. name to any related facility or outside enterprise, lest problems of money, property, and prestige divert us from our primary purpose.

7. Every H.A. group ought to be fully self-supporting, declining outside contributions.

8. Heroin Anonymous should remain forever nonprofessional, but our service centers may employ special workers.

9. H.A., as such, ought never be organized; but we may create service boards or committees directly responsible to those they serve.

10. Heroin Anonymous has no opinion on outside issues; hence the H.A. name ought never be drawn into public controversy.

11. Our public relations policy is based on attraction rather than promotion; we need always maintain personal anonymity at the level of press, radio, and films.

12. Anonymity is the spiritual foundation of all our traditions, ever reminding us to place principles before personalities.

OUR GUIDING PRINCIPLES

*An interpretive summary of the Twelve
Traditions of Heroin Anonymous.*

In the same way our personal recovery is achieved through the Twelve Steps of Heroin Anonymous, the group also has guiding principles embodied in our Twelve Traditions. The group is a spiritual entity, and the Twelve Traditions are the guardrails and effective principles for the group's survival and continued functioning. Our Twelve Concepts for World Service also have practical application at the group level and guide us in protecting the health of the group and the rights of its members.

While all of Heroin Anonymous's principles remain open to individual and group interpretation, valuable experience taught us some foundational lessons captured in our Twelve

Traditions. We learned that the unity and survival of the group had to come first, and that this was even more paramount than the welfare of the individual member. If the group didn't survive, most of us wouldn't be able to find recovery or stay sober ourselves. This was our first and most important tradition. The remaining eleven traditions show us how to keep unified – and continue to live.

We find we are most effective in our primary purpose – staying sober and helping other heroin addicts achieve sobriety – when guided by the group conscience in our business meetings. In a democratic spirit, we try to make important decisions by substantial unanimity whenever possible. By remaining anchored in the principles of Heroin Anonymous, we discern when compromise is needed and when to stand on our convictions. We have faith that God's will is expressed through the informed group conscience, and in instances when the group veers off course, important lessons can be learned and corrective action taken.

We ensure that all voices are heard in our group, even when we disagree. We respect the decisions of the informed group conscience and all members' right to participate. We trust our elected service leaders to perform their duties and lead by example by walking alongside us rather than by mandate. We take no measures to punish anyone and keep close to the principles of love and tolerance. We look to elect the best person for the job, but our service positions also rotate to shield us from believing any one member is too important or indispensable.

We also learned to be inclusive to anyone suffering from heroin addiction – that any heroin or opioid addict has a right to join Heroin Anonymous, regardless of their background or differences. It doesn't matter whether they smoked, sniffed, or injected. No matter what harms they caused or how far down the scale they went in their addiction, we can't keep them out. We only have one requirement: a desire to stop suffering from heroin or opioid addiction. When new people are not sure if they are addicts, we help them discover the truth for themselves and whether H.A. can be helpful to them. We do this by sharing our experience. Our tolerance and gratitude for others goes forward as well as backward, to newcomers and oldtimers alike.

Each Heroin Anonymous group is self-sufficient. Using the Twelve Traditions as guideposts, an H.A. group has the right to function as they decide through their informed group conscience, keeping in mind the individual and group responsibility to avoid actions that could affect other groups or Heroin Anonymous as a whole. When in doubt, we look to the guiding principles in our Twelve Traditions. We also embrace the valuable principle of consulting with other groups and Heroin Anonymous World Services in these matters. We always remember that the purpose of the group is to help the still suffering heroin or opioid addict through the program of Heroin Anonymous as guided by a loving God of our understanding.

We are also cautious of the appearance of affiliation or endorsement, financial or otherwise, with those outside of Heroin Anonymous. We may cooperate with others for the sole purpose of helping the heroin addict through the program of H.A., but we never tie ourselves to them in any way, either actual or implied. Groups reserve the right to create their own customs and formats, but never go into business or own valuable property and instead stick to their primary aim. The temptation for money and influence has to be avoided.

A group of course needs money to pay rent and support themselves, but it should never acquire or keep large sums of money without a stated H.A. purpose. Instead, a group keeps a prudent reserve of funds for the operating costs of their meetings. Rent has to be paid. Meeting materials have to be purchased. An ample reserve should be kept as a safety net so that if contributions fall short, the group can continue carrying the message of Heroin Anonymous. The group should remain poor – but not so poor that it dissolves. (Of course, the group forever remains rich in spirit.) These monies simply enable us to carry the miracle of recovery. Group funds always come from group member contributions and never outside sources; these funds are also never given outside of H.A. Excess monies above the prudent reserve established by the group can be contributed below the group level to Heroin Anonymous service bodies. By making a contribution, we participate, and our participation shows gratitude and acts as an investment in our own and others' sobriety.

Our work with heroin addicts is always most effective when done for free, and our usual 12th Step work is never paid for; we take care to remember that we do not have experts or a professional class of H.A. members. Instead, we give of ourselves, our time, and our experience.

We remember any paid service workers are only making 12th Step work possible for the rest of us, filling a different but vital role. Many members also take service positions below the group level at our districts, areas, regions, committees, and world services to strengthen the link between the groups and Heroin Anonymous as a whole. Intergroups are incorporated separately and remain independent so as to not cause confusion between H.A. and the intergroup's purpose of serving their local needs.

The groups are at the top of our service structure. The other service entities always endeavor to serve the groups and are guided by the Twelve Traditions and Twelve Concepts for World Service of Heroin Anonymous. This repeatedly affirms that good communication within and below the group level promotes even more effective 12th Step work to help the still-suffering heroin or opioid addict at all levels of service. In fact, our elected leaders are expected to be transparent and give good reason for their right to make decisions on our behalf.

Heroin Anonymous is not organized in a traditional way but is structured. Fundamentally, we are lay people, one addict talking to another and sharing experience, strength, and hope. H.A.

is not a corporation, religion, or government and does not have the authority of force. Authority takes the form of trusted responsibility for final decisions. Each individual member and group has the right to exercise H.A.'s principles in their own way without being organized or told how they must practice their 12th Step. Paradoxically, our 9th Tradition guarantees H.A.'s right – and need – to create structure to be effective in carrying the message. These structures should be usable, understandable, and based in our principles. Final responsibility and authority for H.A.'s World Services resides with the collective conscience of the fellowship, and if unity is needed for H.A. to survive, then participation in service is lifegiving for the addict who does not yet know.

We can't be tied to any outside purpose, either. We remain fixed on our sole aim. We carefully avoid publicly expressing any opinions on outside matters, especially controversial ones. It is particularly important for us to steer clear of politics, drug reform, and religion. While members of H.A. have their own individual perspectives on these issues, they are considerate of how these opinions might discourage new people from joining, and these opinions are never expressed publicly as a member or group of Heroin

Anonymous. We recognize that no one member speaks for Heroin Anonymous as a whole.

Additionally, we restrain ourselves by remaining unlinked to outside causes or organizations. To further protect us from ourselves, we do not break our anonymity at the public level, although each member can be as anonymous or open about their membership on an individual basis as they like below this public line. Similarly, we also respect the right of others to be as anonymous as they choose to be without publicly breaking their anonymity. This is the practical application of our personal anonymity. In attracting new members and making others aware of H.A., our society sidesteps taking a sensationalist approach in our relationship to the outside world.

To achieve the ideals contained in our Twelve Traditions as best we can, we are guided by the spiritual application of anonymity in our 12th Tradition. Its spiritual significance is exemplified through humility, sacrifice, and responsibility – the bedrock of our Twelve Traditions. Each of these traditions requires us to remain humble and make individual and group sacrifices. We are responsible to our unity and purpose. As humility, sacrifice, and responsibility are initially necessary for us to achieve our own sobriety, these same principles are also necessary to observe these Twelve Traditions for the individual, the group, and H.A. as a whole.

We place the principles of Heroin Anonymous before our own personalities and give up personal interests, all to support our unity in effectively carrying H.A.'s message of hope, so long as God needs us.

HOW TO GET IN TOUCH WITH H.A.

If you have questions, want to connect with the fellowship, or need support, please get in touch with H.A. We can be reached by mail or by email.

The addresses of various regional representatives and members are below. You can also find additional resources on our website, including meeting kits and H.A. literature, at www. heroinanonymous.org. To write us by mail, please use the following address:

H.A. World Service, Inc.
24 W Camelback Rd.
PO Box 587, Suite A
Phoenix, AZ 85013

Applying to be recognized as a newly-established area or district
hawssecretary@heroinanonymous.org

Adding or editing the meetings listed on the website
hawswebmaster@heroinanonymous.org

Order a free meeting start-up kit
hastartupkits@heroinanonymous.org

Inquire about pending chips and literature orders
hawschipsandlit@heroinanonymous.org

Contact the H.A. Mainline committee
haworldbulletin@gmail.com

Questions about the H.A. World Convention
conventionchair@heroinanonymous.org

Questions about the H.A. World Conference
hawsconferencechair@gmail.com

Information for the General Public and the Professional Community
publicinfo@heroinanonymous.org

For H.A. members looking to connect with the fellowship and get involved in service
hawsoutreach@heroinanonymous.org

Information about Hospitals and Institutions
hawshandi@heroinanonymous.org

For Intellectual Property and Copyright Information
intellectualproperty@heroinanonymous.org

For H.A. members outside of the United States
international@heroinanonymous.org

Regional Trustees

Pacific Regional Trustee
pacificregionaltrustee@heroinanonymous.org

Southwest Regional Trustee
southwestregionaltrustee@heroinanonymous.org

Central Regional Trustee
centralregionaltrustee@heroinanonymous.org

Northeast Regional Trustee
northeastregionaltrustee@heroinanonymous.org

Southeast Regional Trustee
southeastregionaltrustee@heroinanonymous.org

Doughnut Books

www.ingramcontent.com/pod-product-compliance
Lightning Source LLC
Chambersburg PA
CBHW021845130726
47988CB00009B/3423